Praise for The Writetress...

"It is fitting that I'm writing about my experience reading *The Writetress* – on Thanksgiving Day. Why? Because it is one of the most heartfelt books I have ever read. It captures both the wisdom and the challenges one faces as they experientially ascend the ladder of Spiritual Reality. I am thankful for this book. It has my highest recommendation." ~Dr. Ron Hulnick, President of the University of Santa Monica and co-author of *Loyalty To Your Soul: The Heart of Spiritual Psychology*

"Not since Richard Bach's *Illusions* have I read a book so powerful and transformational. *The Writetress* has the potential to change lives". - Dr. Karen M. Bryson, USA TODAY Bestselling Author

"*The Writetress* is a charming read with delightful characters, but that's only the beginning. It is also a shining tale of loving and forgiveness and a set of instructions for living a better life. Simply wonderful fiction that imparts wisdom and grace." - Dayna Dunbar, award-winning author of *Awake: The Legacy of Akara*

"The mysterious plot of *The Writetress* will draw you in. The deep wisdom and powerful spiritual lessons will hold you captive! No doubt, you will find yourself and your life reflected in these pages - and come away transformed." - Don Fergusson, former owner and president of Rust-Oleum Corporation, author of *Salmon to Siddhartha: 5 Vital Principles for an Extraordinary Life*.

The Writetress

A novel by

Lynn Dickinson

This book is dedicated with deep appreciation
to Drs. Ron and Mary Hulnick, who taught
The Writetress everything she knows.

Introduction

Once upon a time, high in the sacred Rocky Mountains of North America, there lived a Writetress. She was a tall, slender woman, slightly older than young, who moved with an effortless grace, whether hiking over the rugged terrain or working in her small garden.

The Writetress was a beloved author of books. Many, many books. Her books spoke of love, the stirring of the soul, the sacred, the universe, and light.

And her books had been published and sold by the millions, in language after language after language. And they touched the consciousness of their readers like nothing else ever written. Many claimed that her words of healing had actually healed, and that her expressions of love and forgiveness had cleansed their readers of previous shortcomings.

And it was written that she was "stunning," and even "breathtaking" in her appearance. In truth, on another, the same face may have been regarded as plain, but there was something about her eyes. Those with something to hide often found her gaze unsettling, as if she could see through them to the core, yet irresistible, as though she loved even those parts inside of them that they couldn't stop hating themselves.

And they called her the "High-Priestess of Writing," which one creative young interviewer had shortened to, "Writetress," many, many years ago. The name had stuck and she had worn it well. Now the world simply knew her as "The Writetress," and most it seemed, had long ago forgotten her real name altogether.

And it came to pass that The Writetress vanished one spring day, revealing her whereabouts to no one. Her publisher could offer no help to the anxious legions of fans and reporters as they began to smell a story. He knew nothing of her whereabouts nor her plans for future books. She had been writing, at her insistence, without a future contract for the last three years and had yet to approach the publishing house with any plans for another book. He had tried to discuss such plans with her last year, but she was not forthcoming with any concrete commitments. No, this wasn't unusual. Yes, they had worked that way before. No, he didn't suspect any foul play – since her checks, forwarded to a private mailbox in New York City, were being cashed, she had recently sent him a birthday card, and after all, it was rumored that she still, occasionally, answered her mail.

The Seeker

"Really? What happened?"

"It was the strangest thing. This woman, Mabel, was coming to the building to visit her daughter, who is my friend, and she got right in the elevator with The Writetress. Mabel didn't even know who she was! I'm not kidding. I guess Mabel doesn't read much. Anyway, The Writetress smiled at Mabel. Then she took off her sunglasses! Right there in the elevator!"

"What happened then?" Derek Shaffer was intrigued. He scratched absentmindedly at a three-day beard and pressed his ear closer to the phone.

"Mabel nearly fainted. She said she'd never felt anything like it. It cured her diabetes you know."

Derek wasn't sure he'd heard that right. "It cured her diabetes?"

"Mabel had diabetes for years before that. Had to take a shot every day. After she looked into The Writetress' eyes, that was it. Never another shot until the day she died four years later. The doctors were amazed."

"Huh."

"Yeah. It was really something. And she was happy after that, too. She went from being a cranky, fat, old diabetic to being a happy, jolly, healthy woman."

"But you don't have any idea where she is now?"

"Mabel? I told you, she's dead."

"No, The Writetress. Where is The Writetress now?"

"Oh, like I said. She's disappeared."

"Do you have any idea how I might be able to locate her?"

"Goodness. No one knows that. You might want to try writing her a letter. They say she still answers her mail sometimes."

"Okay well, thanks."

"And if you find her, please tell her that Maggie Martini in 3G says, "hi" and that the people who bought her old apartment are much too noisy. We'd all like her to come back to the building."

"Will do. Bye now."

Derek hung up the phone and carefully scratched NEIGHBOR NUMBER FOURTEEN off his list. Derek had handled some weird searches in his day, but this one was beginning to get under his skin. He sighed heavily, picked-up the phone again and began dialing.

The Mail

I t arrived at five o'clock, in a black sport utility vehicle with dark windows. The driver coasted to a stop alongside the small wooden mailbox. He turned the tires sharply and set the hand brake against the steep mountain incline, before jumping out of the truck. After depositing three plain, canvas bags filled with letters at the base of the mailbox, he picked up the one, half-full, outgoing bag left for him, and then drove away, back down the hill.

There were no cars visible on the dirt road in either direction when The Writetress reached the bottom of the drive, but then again, there never were. She hoisted one of the bags over her shoulder and started back up the hill without so much as a glance down the steep mountainside toward the not-so-faraway small town.

She moved with an easy self-assurance, hauling the large, canvas sacks up the hill, one at a time, through the thriving aspen grove, toward her modest cabin. Her face moist from exertion, she enjoyed the twice weekly effort. As she trekked up the drive, an occasional sound touched her ears, perhaps some rustle of wildlife or the aspen leaves quaking in a mountain breeze. The sounds always made her smile, but they rarely made her look as she focused on moving her heavy burden further up the hill and away from the road down below.

No one unbidden had ever disturbed The Writetress in her solitude. The cabin was somehow situated so that it was not visible to occupants of cars driving by on the dirt, country road, but nonetheless afforded a generous view of the surrounding mountaintops to its sole human occupant. Were anyone to describe it, they may have said that the cabin seemed to disappear from view, as if by some otherworldly magic, unless The Writetress herself wished it seen. From the road, the only evidence of its presence was the small, weathered, and barely visible mailbox. The box, marked only with the letters A.L. carved neatly, and recently, into the side seemed, like the cabin itself, apparent only to those who were in need of finding it, and had evidently never been noticed by anyone else.

She reached the cabin and paused to catch her breath before negotiating the three wooden steps to the ample, covered front porch. She deposited her cargo next to the empty, bent hickory rocker that swayed now in the breeze. Standing upright she gazed out across the surrounding mountaintops, running her fingers through her loose curls and breathing deeply of the cool air for a moment. Then, steeling her resolve, she started back down the porch steps and the long path down through the aspen, to retrieve yet another bag and repeat her strenuous task again.

After hauling her final sack from roadside to rocker for the day, The Writetress heaved a heavy sigh, and went inside the small, comfortable cabin to make herself a cup of peppermint tea. Steaming mug in hand, she returned to the porch and settled gratefully into the waiting rocker. Regarding the bags at her feet as gently as she might a beloved child, she leaned forward and carefully began releasing the worn, canvas straps that held them closed.

No one person could possibly answer so much mail, but The Writetress had her own personal method for choosing which letters she would attend to. Once all three canvas bags were opened, she sat back in her chair, raised her face heavenward, closed her eyes and inhaled deeply. After a time, she allowed her arm to rise from her lap and guide her attention to the center bag which sat open and waiting.

Once the chosen bag had been identified by some force beyond reason, she took another deep breath, opened her eyes and plunged her hand in, retrieving a nondescript, white envelope from amongst the thousands awaiting her touch. She held it reverently for a moment, and could sense a deep heaviness of Spirit engulfing the very paper of the envelope itself.

While the world eagerly awaited her next book, she now wrote only letters. Where she once penned the occasional article or speech to be read or heard by tens or hundreds of thousands, she now crafted replies directed only to a very few of the specific individuals who had taken the time to write to her first.

What The Writetress now did, it seemed, was to answer her mail.

The Seeker II

Derek hunched over his grimy, paper-strewn desk, absentmindedly nursing a cup of coffee long past its prime and trying to read what little he had on Anika Lucio, aka, The Writetress, again. It was getting dark in New York and he realized he couldn't see a damn thing in the tiny office. He switched on the overhead light which cast a dingy, yellow circle on the desk, but failed to illuminate much of anything. The seven-month-old clipping from the L.A. Times real estate section was worthless anyway. Everyone knew she was gone. Of course, she had sold her California house – and the apartment in New York – and the flat in Paris – the question on everyone's mind was why? And where was she now? Derek intended to find out. One more call wouldn't hurt, he told himself for the eighth, or maybe it was the fifteenth time. He picked up the phone and dialed.

"Coast Realty," the receptionist answered on the third ring.

"Yeah, give me Sandy Sanderson."

"One moment, please."

Even the word "please" was too much for his nerves today and Derek groaned aloud, drumming his fingers rapidly on the desk as his call was being transferred. He badly wanted a cigarette.

"Sandy Sanderson here!" The voice on the other end of the line oozed that maddening perkiness that Derek always found so infuriating in Angelinos. What were they so damn happy about all the time anyway?

"Hi," he did his best to sound civil, if not downright perky himself. "This is Derek Shaffer with the New Jersey Tribune. I'm trying to locate someone you sold a home for a few months ago. My boss wants me to do an interview and I can't seem to track her down."

"Sure. I'll be happy to help if I can," came the bubbly reply. That was one nice thing about perky idiots, they were always happy to help. "Who are you looking for?" she asked.

"Uh, Anika Lucio?" Derek said. An uncertain pause hung on the line. "She's an author. Goes by, The Writetress, I think." Few could play dumb as well as Derek.

"Oh! The Writetress! Of course. She's wonderful!" Sandy was even more enthused and perky. Derek took a deep breath and grabbed a dirty plastic drinking straw to chew on. God, he wanted a cigarette.

"You do know her? Oh good! My boss will be thrilled. Where can I reach her?" His pencil poised itself for the remote possibility.

"Oh, no one knows that!" Sandy said. "She's been missing for months. It's all very mysterious."

"But when she sold her house in Malibu, didn't she leave a forwarding address or something?"

"Oh sure. But it's only a rented mailbox in New York City," explained Sandy. "Lots of people out here are looking for her too, but that's as far as they've gotten. No one knows exactly where she is."

"So, you don't have any idea how I can find her?" Derek pushed.

"Hmmm. Well, you might try writing her a letter. They say she answers her mail sometimes. A friend of mine swears that a friend of hers got a letter just last week! No return ad-dress of course. It's all very mysterious."

"Do you think I could talk to your friend's friend? The one who got the letter? Derek asked

"If you want to see a letter from The Writetress, you could write to her yourself. You never know, she might answer you."

"Okay, maybe I'll try dropping her a line." Derek sighed. "Thanks for your time."

"No problem. I hope you find her. I'd love to see your arti-cle when it comes out. I just love The Writetress, don't you? Her books have totally changed my life."

"Yeah, well. I'll be sure to send you a copy of my piece when it comes out," he lied.

"That would be wonderful. Take care now, and good luck."

"Oh wait!" Derek said. "I just remembered one more thing."

"Sure."

"What can you tell me about her eyes?"

"Oh, her eyes! Oh, wow! Well, they say they're very differ-ent. Supernatural or something, you know? Did you know they can't be photographed?"

"Really? Why not?"

"I don't know. They just never come out right in photo-graphs. All blurry or something. I've heard that some maga-zines just use computers to draw them in for their photos of her."

"You never saw them?"

"Saw her eyes? Me? Oh no!"

"But you must have worked with her when you sold her house."

"Oh, sure I did. I saw her several times. What a great per-son. Always friendly and smiling. It was like she really cared about me as a person, you know? Not like I was just a real estate agent or something."

"How could you work with her and never see her eyes?"

"Oh! She always wears sunglasses."

Derek sighed. "I didn't know that," he lied again.

"I met a guy once who said he saw them."

"Yeah? He saw her eyes? What happened?"

"Well, this guy said he was at a party and The Writetress was there. He could feel her watching him from across the room but he didn't really know who she was. He just thought she liked him; you know?"

"Uh huh."

"Well, he thought she was pretty, which she is by the way. She's very pretty."

"So I've heard." Derek's head was pounding. Cigarette. Cigarette. Cigarette.

"So, he went up to her and introduced himself. When he shook her hand, he said he felt like electricity or something shoot up his arm. He looked up at her and she smiled and took off her sunglasses! Right there at the party! She took them off and looked him right in the eye!"

"And?"

"Well, he wouldn't tell me much more than that, but he did say something like he died a dozen deaths in that moment, or something like that."

Derek forgot his headache. "He said what?"

"He said he died a dozen deaths while she looked into his eyes. And then she put her sunglasses back on."

"What does that mean, he died a dozen deaths?"

"I have no idea; he wouldn't talk about it anymore after that. Seemed like it was a very powerful memory for him."

"I guess so! Who is this guy? Can I talk to him?"

"Oh, I don't really know him that well. I just met him at a bar that one time, you know? I don't even know his name."

"Ah. Okay. Well, thanks for your time."

"Sorry I couldn't be more help. You'll be famous you know."

"Excuse me?"

"If you're the one who finds The Writetress, you'll be famous. Everyone's looking for her. Whoever finds her will be like a contest winner or something."

Derek had actually never thought of that. "Okay. Sure. Huh. Thanks. Take care of yourself. Bye, bye now." Derek nearly gagged on his own words as he hung up the phone. But even though he hadn't gotten what he'd hoped for, he had gotten something. It was a weird something, but something nonetheless. He grabbed his well-chewed pencil and wrote DIED A DOZEN DEATHS in his notepad. Whatever the hell that meant.

He had to stop for the day. The search was going nowhere fast. This Writetress woman had done an amazing job of covering her tracks.

The huge pile of news clippings without photos on his desk was discouraging. Derek didn't believe the wacky eyeball stories for a second, but for a world-famous person who had generated an awful lot of ink, Anika Lucio had certainly done a remarkable job of keeping her face to herself all these years. Even with her coast-hopping, celebrity lifestyle, very few people actually knew what she looked like. She could blend in just about anywhere. Precious little was known about her personal life either. All the public cared about were the stupid books she wrote and how magical she seemed to be. And according to neighbor 14, she could even heal the sick. Sheesh! Derek couldn't fathom how any New Yorker could be so naive and impressionable. An Angelino, sure, but not a New Yorker.

Derek sighed heavily and glanced down at his desk. He picked up a page torn from a three-year-old People magazine. He looked again at the small, grainy, badly-focused picture of Anika smiling out at him from the article. He wasn't one to go in for all this woo-woo, holy woman stuff, but he had to admit, there was something intriguing about her nonetheless.

"Where have you gone, Ms Anika Lucio?" he wondered aloud. "You're quite a smart lady, but I'll find you yet. I don't have a whole lot of choice."

He tossed the page back onto the desk and looked over at the tall stack of pristine, unread Writetress books on the floor in the corner of the cluttered office. Not one of them bore a likeness of the author. It was as though she had been planning her escape for years. "I just hope I don't have to read all those to get what I'm after!" Derek shuddered and turned out the light as he pulled the door shut on the dark room behind him. Then Mr. Derek Shaffer, Private Investigator, went home to sleep. Tomorrow he would begin his search anew.

The Betrayed Woman

Dear Writetress,
I hope you're the one reading this and not just a hired
assistant.

Anika smiled at that one, having at one time not so long ago, employed three different assistants to help her read and respond to each piece of mail.

I'm writing to you because I don't know where else to turn.
I've read all your books, and have given many away as gifts.
They've helped me through some tough times, but this time I
need more help than they can offer.
My husband has had an affair with another woman. I can't
get past the pain and hurt that I feel. I loved and trusted him,
and he betrayed me. Even though I love him, I don't know if I
can ever believe another word he says to me. I don't know what
is wrong with me to have caused him to go outside our marriage.
Maybe she is prettier or younger than I am. We have two young
children. I don't know what to do. Should I leave him or stay
for the sake of the children? Please tell me what you think.
Sincerely,
Kayla Parsons

Anika held Kayla's letter on her lap and gazed out at the mountaintops. There was a storm trying to find its way over the ridge and she watched for a long time before setting pen to paper to craft her reply.

She wrote in the rocker, using a cushioned lap desk, on unique stationery of the highest quality, that she kept nearby in a small pine hutch. Each sheet of paper had been lovingly crafted by hand and bore the mark of a gifted, private artisan. Since making paper of such quality was painstaking work, The Writetress was able to buy every sheet produced by the artisan. He had been well-trained in the spiritual arts and lovingly infused each sheet and matching envelope with a heartfelt essence that could be immediately felt by any sensitive person fortunate enough to hold a piece of this extraordinary work in hand. It was as if the paper was part of the answer to most questions posed by those who wrote to The Writetress, itself a tangible and sublime reminder that there was indeed beauty, love and truth in the world.

The paper artisan produced sheets in a variety of pale earthen and pastel hues from a wide array of materials, so The Writetress was always free to select a sheet that expressed her energy in the moment. She never selected a piece until she had first read a letter and meditated upon her reply.

After quietly holding Kayla's letter for a long while, Anika chose a pale sheet of healing lavender paper, lightly streaked and textured with the raw strips of wood pulp that had given it birth, and began crafting her reply.

—

Dear Kayla,

I can feel the pain in your words and I know you are truly hurting. You feel betrayed, alone, and you're even doubting your own worth and attractiveness. It seems you also feel confused and believe that there is some action you must take to make things right again.

I am honored and humbled that you would write to me for counsel. Although I would never presume to advise you as to what course of action is best for you, perhaps I can be of service in reminding you of a few things which you may have temporarily forgotten in your time of upheaval.

Remember that you are strong. You are loving. And you are wise. You possess a divine inner core that is capable of dealing with any lesson this earth school can throw at you and more. No one can tell you what course of action is best for you, except you. I wish I could tell you how much love I feel for you right at this moment, but I can't do that in person, so this letter will have to suffice. Know that I hold you tenderly in the light and in my thoughts. You <u>can</u> get through this and you will, by holding loving thoughts for yourself and forgiving thoughts for both yourself and for those who have hurt you. I will remember you in my meditations where I shall always see you as the strong, vibrant, divine and perfect being I know you to be.

Please remember to:

Acknowledge what is,

Accept what is,

And respond to what is, with love.

Yours in the light,

W.

To be certain, those of a more critical nature might scoff at the gentle reply. "Tell her to leave the bum!" they might insist. "Tell them to kiss and make up," others might advise. But those detractors would never experience the letter written only for Kayla's eyes. And miraculously, a week and a half later, a troubled young woman a thousand miles away would retrieve her mail and notice the unusual lavender envelope amongst the daily pile of bills and catalogs. She would hold it in her hand, feeling a sense of wonder wash over her as her eyes traced the beautiful lettering that spelled out her name. For a moment, everything else would be forgotten as the woman, gazing curiously at the envelope, pondered who it could possibly be from.

She would absentmindedly set about making herself a cup of tea and would settle in on the worn sofa in her tiny apartment all alone with the beautiful envelope. Her envelope. She would never see another like it in her life. Slowly, carefully, she would slide a knife under the flap, taking care to slice the top cleanly, leaving no unnecessary disturbances in the fold, and retrieve the matching sheet from within. Marveling first at the elegant flow of the handwriting, her eyes would be drawn to the mark of The Writetress that graced the top of the page and she would gasp at the realization that she held in her hand the letter she herself had requested in desperation, some three weeks earlier.

As she read, tears would flow. Tears of relief at having someone actually understand what she was going through. Tears of awe that someone could think of her in such a tender and loving way. Tears of amazement that someone as well-known and esteemed as The Writetress would share her precious time and energy with a troubled housewife from the middle of nowhere whose plea for help could have much more easily been ignored.

Although Kayla's troubles would not end immediately on that day, receiving such a caring note from such an important person would mark a turning point for her. From that day forward, she would seem to walk a little taller and smile a little more often. She would cry a lot less and when she did, her tears would be those of healing and forgiveness. She would return to that letter again and again throughout the remainder of her life, in good times and in bad, and it would become one of her most cherished possessions. She would never breathe a word about it to another soul and she would keep it carefully hidden, to be discovered only by her children years later when sorting through her meager belongings after her death.

And although The Writetress would never know what effect this or that letter might have on someone like Kayla – she had faith in her beliefs and in herself, and had decided of late that this was to be her ministry.

And so, she wrote.

Healing

On this clear, Autumn afternoon when she finished writing her reply to Kayla, Anika sat quietly, sealed envelope in hand, blessing it with her loving energy and praying that her reply would be helpful. Then she turned her awareness inward and began searching for any place or places within herself that resonated with Kayla's letter.

Anika knew that any letter she selected while in a guided state could hold a message or learning for her, as well as for the person who had written it. Today she began by searching within herself for any unresolved issues of betrayal and found none. She had certainly known betrayal in her life, having at one time had a trusted financial advisor who had robbed her of all income from her first two books. She had experienced the betrayal of confidences as well, when on occasion, things she said or did in intimate settings were leaked to the press and published for all to see. And there were others, too. But she had forgiven her betrayers each time and forgiven herself for judging herself as a victim each time, to the point where each instance of betrayal that she could recall yielded no real disturbance of her peace with its memory.

So, she moved on in her inner search, questing after that as yet unresolved issue that she felt Kayla's letter trying to show her. Was it confusion or indecision? No, Anika had always been strongly decisive and had never developed the troublesome habit of looking back or second guessing herself. It wasn't that.

What about worth? Could Kayla's letter be telling The Writetress that something was as yet unresolved within herself around the issue of self-worth? Anika listened and felt the smallest ripple of emotion somewhere deep inside of her and knew she had found her purpose in the letter she had just answered. She let her mind drift back to times when she doubted her own worth as a person and as a writer.

She had always known she was born to write, but for some reason, hadn't set pen to paper until she was nearly thirty-five years old. The instant she started publishing, all doubts as to her writing abilities had apparently vanished and her life and career had kicked into high gear. She had never taken the time to go back and explore what those first years of being a non-writing writer meant to her. Today she concluded that she hadn't felt a confidence in the value of her words or her voice. She knew now that she was afraid then. She knew that there was a part of her, however small, that still lived with that doubt, and finding that part caused her to smile for joy at the opportunity to heal this issue for the last time.

Anika didn't answer any more letters that day. She spent the rest of that afternoon and evening praying and working to heal the part of her that still had some doubt as to her worth as a writer. She sat on the porch and gazed at the sunset as she acknowledged and accepted the aspects within her that had kept her from publishing sooner. She worked to appreciate those inner, subconscious qualms which were, after all, only trying to protect her from what she had fantasized would be sure rejection. She built a lively fire in the living room as she practiced forgiving herself for ever doubting herself and her abilities. As she chopped fresh carrots and broccoli for her evening meal, she worked to reframe her inner issues and redefine them with her current perspective – that of a wildly successful writer.

As Anika finished her meal that evening, she thanked Spirit for bringing the day's issue to light for her to examine and heal, and acknowledged herself for her own willingness to work it out. She knew it would be easiest to simply deny her own unresolved issues and pretend they didn't exist, as so many of those regarded as popular gurus had done before her, so she valued her own eagerness and strength to work with those particular quirks and lessons that rightfully belonged to her.

In her own way, The Writetress was reaching out to the world of people one-by-one, while she identified and healed her own corresponding, inner issues one-by-one. It had become her quest. And so tonight she dined on homemade vegetable soup with a thick slab of fresh bread. Tomorrow she would read another letter.

On this particular night, when she felt complete with her process and was confident that she had truly healed something within herself, Anika felt a strong desire to connect with someone. She decided to write to Corinne.

—

Hi Honey,

I hope you are well. Much has changed since I last wrote to you about the cabin. It grows more and more my own each day. The aspen are just beginning to turn and the surroundings are perfect. I'm eager for you to visit soon. I hope you'll teach me a few new recipes, since I'm growing rather weary of my own limited kitchen repertoire.

I'm adjusting well to life without lattés, but I still miss my massages and manicures. I was, I'll admit, quite pampered. But not anymore. I'm still hoping to wake up one morning and find myself completely enlightened, as so many seem to think I already am, but at the moment I'm still working out the kinks and it does get lonely up here sometimes.

Please come visit me soon.

I love you with all my heart,
Mom

The Seeker III

Derek woke up with a headache. Someone was pounding loudly on the door of his tiny, Brooklyn apartment.

"Hang on, hang on," he yelled as he did an unpleasant slapstick routine trying to get his pants on. "What?" he hollered through the door.

"Open up, it's me," came the familiar voice.

Derek opened up the door, "I hope you brought – "

Jack handed Derek a paper cup. "Coffee," they both finished together.

"I wouldn't arrive here before nine without coffee, Boss," said Jack. "I might be stupid but I'm not an idiot." He looked around the room, "Impressive mess. Did we have an earthquake nobody told me about? Where's Cassandra?"

"Shut up," Derek grumbled as he finished getting dressed. "You know damn well she's gone. And don't call me Boss! You're two years older than I am, for Christ's sake! You got a cigarette?"

Jack fished around in his pocket. "I just thought, you know, she'd be back by now. She's usually back by now, ain't she?" He produced a crumpled cigarette and a grungy disposable lighter. "I thought you quit."

"She says it's for real this time. She ain't coming back." Derek lit the cigarette and inhaled the smoke deeply. He shook his head in disbelief. "I don't know why I ever wanted to give these up. Man! What was I thinking?"

Jack shrugged as Derek savored the smoke. "Where'd she go?"

"I dunno. To her mom's or something."

"You gonna go get her?"

"Nope." Derek inhaled again. "God, this is a good cigarette. What brand are these? I'm gonna switch."

"I dunno, Camels maybe? I bummed 'em off Shakey Bill down at Earl's. How come you're not gonna go after her this time?"

Derek shrugged. "It's over, Jack. She's too much like my dad. She doesn't want me around until I make something of myself, and from the looks of things, that ain't gonna happen anytime soon. Besides, I got a new client. Big one. Big job. Missing Person."

"Yeah?"

"Yep. It's taking all my time and then some, but . . ." Derek rubbed his fingers against his thumb, "we're talking major moolah here."

"Yeah? Who you after?"

"Anika Lucio. Goes by The Writetress. Ever heard of her?"

Jack scratched his head. "Ain't she that famous writer that's gone missing?"

"Bingo. Some people think she's magical or something too."

"Magical?"

"Yeah, like she can heal the sick or do funny things to people with her eyes."

Jack looked uncomfortable. "What kind of funny things?"

"What difference does it make? None of its true anyway. Just a bunch of stupid people thinking she's some kind of holy woman or something."

"Wait a minute. Isn't like, everyone and their uncle looking for her?" Jack asked.

"Yeah, so?"

"So, what makes you think you're gonna be the one to find her?"

"'Cause I need the money more than anyone else."

"We all need money, Derek."

"Yeah, but I got inside information. My client knows things about her. I got full name, DOB, last known addresses, everything."

"Then where is she?"

"I haven't exactly figured that out. She's got business managers paying her bills, her assets are hidden in a bunch of different trusts, and she uses a mail drop in mid-town. But I got three months to find her."

"Wow. Sounds tough. How you gonna do it?"

"I'm still working out my plan. I'm going up to the city today. Maybe I can get the guy at the mail drop to tell me something."

"Ha! Good luck with that!" Jack scoffed. "Want me to come with you?"

"Aren't you working on that Maggini case?"

"Yeah, but that's boring. Just some guy thinks his wife is cheating on him. You know, the usual."

"Is she cheating on him?"

"I dunno. You just gave it to me three days ago."

"Yeah, well wrap it up quick. This one is big and I might need you to take some of my other cases or something.

"You got other cases?"

"Not yet. But this one is definitely big. I might need you to take all my new cases while I keep working on this one. Got it?"

Jack laughed, "Derek, you've been giving me every new client you've gotten for the past two months. Your old man, finally, after five years of not talking to you, says it's okay with him if you want to be a dick, and you suddenly decide you don't want to be one anymore."

Jack shook his head. "So why you suddenly keeping this job to yourself? You said you were gonna do something else with your life."

"Yeah, well I haven't thought of anything else yet. At least not anything that he'll really hate." Derek grinned to himself. "And in the meantime, this client comes along and forks over a big cash advance. See?"

Derek held out a wad of bills. Jack whistled low. "And there's more where that came from, long as I can find her. So, I'm back in the biz for now."

"So, who's the client?" Jack's eyes were still on the money.

"Can't tell you that." Derek pocketed the cash.

"Why not? He's not some loopy stalker after the famous writer or something, I hope."

"No." Derek was insulted. "Come on. What do you think I am?

"Sorry, Boss."

"Damn right you're sorry."

"So, who is he then?"

"I told you! I can't tell you."

"Why not? I'm your partner, remember? You said as soon as I got my license, we were gonna be partners."

"I know what I said, but you don't have your license yet, remember?"

Jack looked hurt. Derek tried to make amends. "Look, this client told me not to tell. If I tell anybody, that's it! No more deal. I ain't blowing this one. Not this one. This one is way too big."

"Well why does he wanna find her in the first place? Is she an old flame of his or something?"

"No, nothing like that."

"What? She owe him money or something?"

"No! It's just a simple delivery."

"What? A process serving gig?"

"No! Stop asking me about my client! I ain't talking about my client. Not with you, not with nobody. Not until I find this wacko, guru, holy person, whatever-the-hell-she-is, and prove to the world that Derek Shaffer really is a damn good P.I. after all."

"Even if being a P.I. stinks?"

"Even if being a P.I. stinks. Which it does."

"Well at least you made rent then, huh?" Jack looked around the grubby apartment again.

"Yeah, well, thing is, I kinda need to use this money to find this woman. There might be some expenses involved, you know? After I find her, we're talking big bucks, but right now . . . I just can't."

Jack looked around, understanding. He stood to leave. "Okay, well, you know you can crash at my place. Anytime. If you need to, you know?"

"Thanks, Jack. You're a pal. I've still got a few days to pay up. Maybe I can find her by then. Don't worry. I'm good." The two men stood silently for an awkward beat, then Derek grabbed his Knicks cap. "Let's get going. I gotta see a man about a mailbox!"

They left the apartment, closed the door behind them and started down the dingy hallway. They walked in silence for a few steps, then Derek remembered something.

"Hey, You know what, Jack?"

"What?"

"After I find this lady, I'm gonna be famous."

"Yeah?"

"Everyone will pay me, Derek Shaffer, to tell 'em where she is. Not just my client. Everyone."

"Huh."

"Things are gonna be different around here from now on. A lot different."

"Yep."

"I might never have to work again."

"Yep."

"Got another cigarette?"

"Uh huh."

The Fan

Having slept a dreamless night, Anika awoke with the morning birdsong to her regular, simple yoga practice. She ate a light breakfast indoors at her rough-hewn, wooden table and offered a bowl of milk to the little black and white cat who provided her good company some of the time. Afterward, she felt refreshed and alert enough to return to her porch and this week's sack of letters.

After the usual meditation and request for guidance, she chose another letter and began to read.

Dear Writetress,

I've not written to a celebrity before, so I'm not sure what to say. I don't want to take up too much of your time.

I just wanted you to know how much I love your work. You are a truly gifted and blessed writer. I always feel so tongue-tied when I try to explain my beliefs about spiritual matters to people. I can never seem to get it right. But you express things so eloquently. Your books have changed my life and I wanted to thank you for writing them.

Love,

Frank Harris

Anika smiled as she selected a pale, yellow sheet of paper for her reply to Frank.

—

Dear Frank,

Thank you for your kind letter. I am moved to know that I have contributed, in some small way, to your life. Please remember that you can only recognize in others the qualities that you yourself already possess deep within (although you may not have yet fully realized or taken ownership of them). If they weren't inside you, you would not be able to see them in me. I invite you to look inward, to your true divine core, and find those abilities within you that resonate with the qualities you admire in me and my work. They are yours to claim for yourself. Now that we have shared this correspondence, I will remember you in my meditations and hold you always in the light.

Please remember to:
Acknowledge what is,
Accept what is,
And respond to what is, with love.
Yours in the light,
W.

Once Anika had sealed her simple reply, she gave herself freedom to reflect on the larger matter that had just been presented to her. On the one hand, she could take Frank's kind words and experience them as flattering. She could choose to feel good about them and apply their loving energy as a kind of balm to her own inner sense of lack. But The Writetress knew, as had other great spiritual teachers before her, that she would only be kidding herself if she were to take another's words as accurate reflections of herself. Whether those words be kind or unkind, they could only be mere reflections of another person's perceptions, and not of any true reality about the being presently known as Anika.

The Seeker IV

Times Square was more crowded than Derek remembered it. It took a long time to find the mailbox place, and when he finally spotted it from the other side of 47th, it was still, for some reason, tough to get a bead on as he crossed the street. It took him three tries to find the tiny doorway. Three times crossing back to the other side of the street and searching, finally spotting it, crossing back and then trying to find it again up close. It was as if the damn thing moved or just plain disappeared whenever Derek took his eyes off of it long enough to navigate a crossing. He was not having fun.

At last he found himself standing directly in front of the dark doorway, and decided to fortify himself with a cigarette before going in. He leaned up against the wall to smoke and tried peering inside through the thick glass, but couldn't see a thing. He heaved a heavy sigh, tossed his cigarette butt on the ground, stubbed it out with his sneaker, and tried to come up with a plan. He'd never had much luck getting mail drop guys to sing. They were notorious for keeping quiet about their clients, but it was the only lead he had at the moment so he tried to think of a decent scam.

As Derek looked around, he noticed a deli counter with a rack of flowers for sale out front, just two doors down from where he was standing. It was as good a ruse as any. At first, he was half afraid to take the twenty or thirty steps needed to get there. Half afraid he'd not be able to find the mail drop again when he returned. *What am I, nuts?* Derek shook off the idea that an entire shop could disappear at will and headed toward the florist, counting his steps and looking behind him every so often just to be sure. He blew some of his client's cash on a bouquet, sealed a blank card into an envelope, wrote "Anika" on the outside, and headed back to the mail drop. The place was still there but there was definitely something hinky about it.

A bell rang on the door as he opened it and stepped into the dim interior. In the moment it took his eyes to adjust, he saw he was standing alone in a lobby filled with mailboxes. He heard a bustling from behind the counter at the other end of the lobby and a dark, little man responding to the sound of the bell, came out from the back room.

"How is it I can help you?" he asked.

Derek tried to look surprised that he was standing in a box rental shop. He held up the flowers. "Delivery for Ms Anika Lucio, but this can't be the right address." He pulled a notepad from his pocket and pretended to check some illegible notes as if verifying for himself that this was indeed the place.

The little man reached out to take the flowers. "I will be taking them for her."

Derek hesitated. "Uh, I'm supposed to give them only to Ms Lucio, you know? My boss'll have my hide if I give 'em to you. Can you just tell me where she lives so I can deliver them while they're still fresh?"

"Oh no. I will not be falling for that trick," said the little man, pointing to a large sign on the wall behind him that Derek only just now noticed. It read, "No Questions Answered. No Boxes Available."

"What does that mean, no questions answered?" Derek asked.

"It means what it says. It means I will not be cooperating with you or with any of the others who are looking for my friend."

"Ah! So, you do know her?"

"Of course, I know her! She is my good customer. Now it is time for you to be leaving." He came out from behind the counter to show Derek to the door.

"Wait a minute." His cover totally blown, Derek tried to buy some time.

"No! There is nothing I will be telling you!" The little fellow was getting agitated. "Give me those." He grabbed the flowers from Derek and slapped them on the counter. "And get out of my store."

"Okay, okay," said Derek, backing away with his hands up in a placating gesture. "Just tell me this one thing: why don't you have any boxes available for rent?"

"Because I am all sold out. They are all being rented now. That is why."

"But there's nobody in here." Derek whirled around. "There's never anybody in here – is there?"

"I'm sorry, but all my boxes are rented just now. You may go."

The little man started out from behind the counter to open the door for Derek. Derek tried to stall his exit. "What? Is she your *only* customer? Does she rent all the boxes in this place?"

"Thank you for coming. Do not come back please." They were almost to the door.

"There must be five hundred boxes in here!"

"Five hundred and twenty-two."

"Are you telling me one person rents five hundred and twenty-two boxes?" The little man didn't answer. Instead, he pushed open the door and began shoving Derek out. One last desperate thought occurred to Derek.

"Hey! Have you ever seen her eyes?"

The little man froze in his tracks. He looked stunned, as though Derek had pulled a gun. For a moment, he seemed to be transported to somewhere else, breathing heavily and saying nothing. There was a look of great longing on his face, as though he had lost something once very precious and dear to him. After a moment something snapped inside the man and he fixed his eyes coldly on Derek. His face contorted in anger.

"What do you know of her eyes?" he hissed. His own eyes traveled over Derek as though he were surveying a cockroach. "What does someone like . . . like you, know about her eyes?"

"Nothing, I . . ."

"That is right. Unless you have seen them yourself, as I have, you know nothing! Remember that! You know nothing! Now go!" The man pushed Derek over the transom and forced the door shut behind him. "You know nothing!" he shouted, and locked the door solidly.

"Locking up so early?" Derek shouted through the glass. "What if you get a customer?"

Derek slumped against the wall, dejected. "You know nothing!" he mocked the little man aloud. A passing Japanese tourist grinned hugely at this, nodded eagerly and said, "You know nothing? You know nothing?" Derek shook his head in disbelief. The Japanese man continued practicing his handy new English phrase as he disappeared into the crowd. The entire world was definitely askew. Derek sighed heavily and reached for a cigarette.

The Old Woman

Dear Writetress,

    I am 87 years old and I have lived too long. My body hurts, my friends are all dead, I can't hear, and I know that my mind is beginning to slip. I can't drive anymore. I can't even do my own housework, cook my own meals, or take my own medicine without assistance. I have a helper that comes to my house to take care of me as if I were a child. I am a burden to my grown children who have busy lives and children of their own to worry about. I don't want to be alive anymore. I wish I could just die and be with my late husband and friends again. Why has God let me live so damn long? Why doesn't he just take me? The doctors say I am healthy and may live for many more years and that news just makes me more depressed. I am of no earthly use to anyone anymore. Why am I still here?

    Sincerely,
Evelyn Johnson

—

Dear Evelyn,

    Thank you for writing to me. It is an honor and a privilege to hear from one who has seen so many years go by and so many changes take place in the world. I hear that you are tired and depressed and feeling like a burden to your family.

You say that there is no earthly reason for you to be here anymore and you may be right. There probably is no earthly reason. But know this: none of us are really here for any <u>earthly</u> reason. Since we are all divine souls simply having a human experience for a while, our reasons for being here are entirely Spiritual. We may forget that in the hustle and bustle illusions of everyday living, but it remains true nonetheless. Removed as you are from the busyness of the world around you, you now have a blessed opportunity to remember what is truly important.

You are here because you are meant to be. You are here for your own highest good and the highest good of all concerned. We can't always know Spirit's reasoning for things, but I can assure you that you are providing some benefit to your family, to your helper, and to yourself by being here — of that I am 100% certain. Perhaps this situation was designed by God to provide your children the opportunity for learning forgiveness, compassion, patience, caring or just a new level of appreciation and gratitude for their own health and family. Perhaps your helper is practicing skills of giving, commitment, service, responsibility, loving or caring for another while earning an income. Perhaps you too, have an opportunity to practice graciousness, receiving, forgiveness, gratitude and loving in the face of a trying situation.

You can add to the sum total of love in the world or you can add to the sum total of anger and frustration — but either way — you do have an impact — just as we all do. I encourage you to spend your remaining days on earth in the loving. Choose gratitude over frustration, caring and appreciation for others over annoyance at being cared for, and forgiveness over judgment for your situation. Appreciate whatever opportunities you still have to contribute to the lives of those around you — even if those contributions don't look the way you've always imagined they should. Remember that asking for, and graciously receiving help are valuable contributions to others as well. They provide opportunities for another soul to grow and be generous in loving and giving. I for one, am glad you're here. Thank you, Evelyn.

Please remember to:
Acknowledge what is,
Accept what is,
And respond to what is, with love.
Yours in the light,
W.

The Seeker V

A light rain was keeping the evening crowds at bay in midtown for the moment. After pacing up and down 47th for awhile, doing his best to keep a solid eye on the little shop where Anika Lucio got her mail, Derek had stubbornly taken up residence in the window seat of a coffee shop across the street. He had been sitting there for hours, within view of the strange little store, just to test his theory. It was exactly as he expected. Not one customer had entered or left the shop all day long. The sole visitor to the place was the mail carrier, who double parked his USPS truck in front, unloaded a couple of obviously full mail bags, and dragged them up to the front door. The dark little man inside was already waiting at the open door to claim them. Once he had possession of the bags and the mail carrier had departed empty handed, the little man glanced furtively up and down the street and withdrew back inside with his prize, locking the door again behind him. Not a soul seemed to notice the place otherwise.

Derek's phone rang in his pocket as the large waitress poured yet another cup.

"You wanna eat something, honey?" she asked as Derek fumbled for his cell.

"Uh, no, not right now." She didn't budge. He checked the look on her face and quickly changed his mind as the phone rang again. "Okay, why don't you just bring me a menu then?"

"You got one right there," she gestured at the tabletop with the eraser end of her pencil. She still didn't budge. The phone rang a third time.

"Okay, just let me get this and I'll order something. I promise." The waitress retreated warily, keeping an eye on Derek as he answered the call.

"Derek Shaffer here."

"Oh. Uh, hi. Is this the New Jersey Tribune?" There was something familiarly irritating about the voice. Derek stopped himself from a quick wrong number disconnect.

"Uh, who are you trying to reach?"

"There's a reporter there looking for The Writetress. I can't remember his name. He called here yesterday afternoon."

"Oh, yeah! Hi! This is me, Derek. This is my cell phone number. It's . . .uh," Derek flipped quickly through his notebook, "Sandy, right?"

"Yeah, Sandy Sanderson in L.A. Remember? I sold The Writetress' house in Malibu last Spring."

"Yeah, hi. Did you have something else to tell me about The Writetress?"

"Well, you asked about my friend's friend who got a letter from her."

"Yeah?"

"Well, she doesn't want to show it to you. She said she doesn't want anyone to see it or touch it or anything. It's special, you know?"

"Oh. Okay. Well then, uh . . . thanks for calling."

"But she did say there was a postmark on the envelope."

Derek perked up immediately. "Really? A postmark? Where from?"

"It was posted in Marina Del Rey. That's right near here! I think The Writetress is somewhere out here. Isn't that just the greatest thing you ever heard?"

"That is really interesting, yeah. Hey, thanks!"

"No problem. If I hear anything else about The Writetress, do you want me to call you?"

"Definitely. I'd really appreciate it, in fact."

"Okay, I will. I gotta call Paul now and tell him too."

"Paul?"

"He's a real, honest-to-goodness Private Eye! He lives out here and he's looking for The Writetress too! Can you believe it?"

"Paul? Paul who?"

"I don't know. He never told me his last name. Isn't that funny? He called me last week. It's just so cool that I get to help a real reporter *and* a real Private Eye!"

Derek squirmed uncomfortably. "Yeah, well yeah, that's pretty cool. Uh, did he say why he was looking for her?"

"Oh, don't worry. He's not planning to write a competing story or anything. He won't 'scoop' you," Sandy giggled. "He just said he had something to deliver to The Writetress for a client of his."

"Oh?"

"But I think he wants to be famous for being the one who finds her too. Hey! Maybe all three of us will find her together! Wouldn't that be a hoot? We can all be famous!"

"That would be a hoot all right." Derek desperately wanted the conversation to end. Now.

"I'm going to a club in the Marina tonight," Sandy fairly squealed. "I'll keep my eyes and ears open. This is so exciting!"

"Yeah. Great. Thanks. Wow. Yeah. Bye now."

Derek hung up the cell, intrigued and troubled by what he had just heard. *So, her mail comes from Marina Del Rey*, Derek thought, *and someone else has a delivery for her too.* Who could it be? He suspected that time was running out for him on this job. Was he competing with another P.I. on behalf of the same client? Was he competing with several? That just plain sucked. Not only did he have to find the world's most invisible holy woman for this paycheck, but he had to do it before God only knew how many others with the same motivation and inside information.

Derek began jotting a reminder to himself to check into Private Detectives named Paul in Los Angeles, when he felt the hair on the back of his neck slowly stand straight up. Derek froze. All his experience and instincts told him he was in trouble. He became acutely aware that he was being closely watched by someone on the other side of the room.

Adrenaline pumping, he took a couple slow, deep breaths, faked a yawn, and nonchalantly leaned back against the chair. Slowly he turned his gaze in toward the crowded restaurant, scanning the faces of the other diners, casually seeking his pursuer.

The instant his eyes met hers, she started straight toward him at full speed. Derek snapped to attention in his seat, and pressed back hard against the chair in an instinctive but futile effort to hide. His eyes widened as he groped blindly for something on the tabletop but to no avail. Then his mind snapped with a sure-fire strategy. "Just gimme a grilled cheese sandwich," he blurted in a brilliant move of self-defense. She veered instantly toward the kitchen in retreat. Derek exhaled a sharp, short sigh of victory and shook off the tension. Crisis averted, he congratulated himself. He decided to celebrate with a cigarette while waiting for his food.

The Cancer

Dear Writetress,

I have been told that I have breast cancer and my doctor says it is likely to be fatal. I fear I have never really lived and now I am soon going to die. I don't even know what to feel. Sometimes I am angry and sometimes I am so depressed I can barely move. What should I do? Please help me.

Sincerely,
Catherine Northsrom

—

Dear Catherine,

There are many lessons to be learned here on this physical plane, and sometimes they are truly painful. It is a very natural and human thing to feel anger and depression in the face of such a momentous change. But please know this: although pain seems a mandatory part of our human experience, _suffering_ is entirely optional. Whatever Spirit has planned for you, please trust that it is in your best interests and for your highest good. I know that can be difficult to accept in times like this, but I believe it to be true with all my heart.

We all live and we all die and we all live again. We can assume there is some purpose to all this nonsense, but only at our divine, inner core, do we truly know what we are here to accomplish. I'm confident that whatever it is, it has something to do with experiencing and expressing pure love, compassion, acceptance and joy.

I urge you to look within yourself — to that place inside you that is connected with Spirit — and find the answer to your own question. It is to be found there, and no place else, I assure you.

If you so desire, you may choose to remain angry and depressed until the day you die and no one would blame you a bit. It is a legitimate choice. If you prefer, however, to exercise some other options, ask your divine Self what it is you want to learn before you leave this life and then trust that answer. Ask what it is you came here to contribute and then trust that truth as well. Act on your findings. Now.

In truth, you have been given a gift: a reminder that life is short. Not one among us has been promised tomorrow, but mostly we forget that. We proceed through our lives, postponing our true passions, as though we had all the time in the world. I urge you to use your impending death as an ally to keep you focused on what it is you truly want to leave behind. So many people find their lives suddenly over, while they were still waiting for them to begin. You have been given an opportunity to avoid making that same mistake. I urge you to take it. Make choices now that will serve you well forever.

I will keep you in my healing meditations.

Please remember to:

Acknowledge what is,

Accept what is,

And respond to what is, with love.

Yours in the light,

W.

—

My Dearest Kitten,

    I was just blessed with a reminder that life is short and wanted to use this precious moment of mine, to tell you how much I love you and miss you. Thank you for being my daughter.

    Love,
    Mom

The Wood Man

Anika remembered the first time she saw him. He drove up with the load of wood she had ordered, and got out of the truck in front of her house, pulling on his canvas work gloves as he walked toward the tailgate of the battered pickup. She remembered registering an initial reaction of surprise at the sight of the short, stocky man with the straight hair, slack jaw and slightly open mouth.

Anika had never personally known anyone with severe mental disabilities before she met Danny. She was surprised he could drive, and thought that maybe, if he lived in the city, he wouldn't have had such freedom.

It occurred to Anika, that if they both lived in the city, their paths might cross daily but they would never get to know one another. Danny would have been one of the invisible people. One of the millions who toil in service as they live and breathe undetected in the shadows of the more hierarchically conscious.

Anika loved to sit in her rocker and watch Danny work as he stacked her wood onto the pile at the far end of the porch. He was probably in his late twenties and always wore baggy, faded jeans and a plain white t-shirt, regardless of the weather. He was extremely conscientious in his task. She marveled at how hard he labored, yet how relaxed and centered he seemed. While others may only have seen a simpleton struggling with a basic task, if they noticed Danny at all, Anika looked more deeply and saw much more.

He worked slowly and methodically, taking only one or two very specific logs from the back of the truck at a time and stacking them with artistic precision and unflagging attention to detail. He always took extra care to arrange the best firewood on top of the orderly pile for her. He would also refill the kindling bucket every time and thoroughly sweep the front porch clean of woodchips, even though Anika had not requested such service.

It struck Anika that Danny was the epitome of mindfulness at work. He performed his labors with a careful and focused consciousness that could only be described as loving. He appeared to be wholly present and fully absorbed in his humble task of providing service for another human being. He worked with a grace and ease that most people only rarely encounter in their lives, and Anika felt fortunate for the opportunity to be in his presence for a short time each month.

The first time Danny came, Anika offered him a cold glass of lemonade when he was finished. Danny nodded and wiped his sweaty forehead with the back of a dirty glove. He stood silently on the porch waiting until she beckoned him to follow her into the house. As he waited in the living room, Anika opened the refrigerator. When she turned around to pour the drink, Danny was gone. She didn't have long to be puzzled however, since he announced his return with a loud bang, kicking open the front door, his arms loaded with wood. He had noticed the dwindling pile of logs on her stone hearth and decided to replenish that supply as well. Then he gulped his lemonade in a silence that seemed perfectly natural to them both, nodded to Anika and was gone, back into his pickup truck and back down the driveway until next time.

As the months passed, they established their routine. Anika sitting on the porch writing letters or watching until Danny was finished stacking wood. When he was done, Danny would stand quietly by her chair with an armload of wood until she noticed him and let him inside to renew the pile by the hearth. Then he would drink the lemonade that Anika always took care to have prepared for him, and leave. They had never spoken, yet an unmistakable bond had formed.

The Seeker VI

Derek finished the last of his fries just as the lights began to come on in Times Square. He wiped his mouth with the frayed remains of an undersized paper napkin and sighed contentedly. But before he could even light up a cigarette, the waitress from hell was back. With one practiced move, she swept the plate from the table, slapped down his final check, and turned toward the kitchen. Derek was annoyed.

"Hey. Aren't you even gonna ask me if I want dessert?" he shouted at the retreating form.

She stopped in her tracks and turned slowly around. He hadn't reckoned on her actually taking the bait. This was, after all, a very big woman. Another test. Derek readied himself for the challenge. He liked to test his daring whenever the opportunity presented itself, however pathetic that opportunity might be.

"You want dessert?" She looked him square in the eye

"No." he replied with an equally steady gaze.

She glared. Derek glared back. Time stood still before she shook her head in disgust and returned her body to its original kitchenward trajectory. Derek smiled a satisfied smile for just a beat, and then shook his head. *I gotta stop doing that*, he thought.

Back outside, Derek shivered in the late September twilight. Other than the regular postal delivery, nothing at all had happened at the little mailbox place all day. Derek leaned against the wall outside the café, had a smoke, kept watch across the street, and amused himself by chanting "Waitress, Writetress, Waitress, Writetress," for a while. In half an hour, the mail drop would close for the day and he could go home. It hardly seemed worth the wait.

His phone rang and he answered it where he stood, never taking his eyes off the store.

"Derek Shaffer here."

"Derek, it's me. Jack."

"Jack, hey. What's up?"

"I was just calling to see how the big search was going. Get anything good on The Writetress today?"

"Don't call her that. Her name is Anika Lucio. Only idiots call her The Writetress. It's stupid. Sounds like waitress or something."

"Okay, okay. Sorry. You get anything on her today?"

"Not much. I did find out she rents a mailbox place here in mid-town."

"I thought you already knew she had a box there.

"Not a box. She rents the whole store! I think she's their only customer!"

"Jeez! That's gotta cost a lot of money."

"Yeah, well she's got a lot of money. And I think she's using a fair amount of it to hide herself."

"Guess so! Hey, I wrapped that Maggini case today, just like you said."

"Really? Was she cheating on him?"

"Sure, she was. That's why it was so easy to wrap."

"Great. Well, I might need you to come up here with me tomorrow and stake out the back door. What goes in must come out, as they say. Hey . . . Wait a minute . . ."

"Gee, Derek, that'd be great. I'd love to. . ."

"Hold on, Jack! Wait!"

The door of the shop had opened and the little man was peering cautiously up and down the street. Derek quickly hid himself behind a lamppost. He hissed into his phone.

"There's something going on here. Wait."

"I'm with you, Buddy. I'm holding."

Derek watched quietly. When he seemed satisfied that the coast was clear, the little man stepped out onto the walk and waved once down the street as though he were hailing an invisible taxi. Within seconds a large black sedan with dark windows pulled up out of nowhere and stopped in front of the box shop. The driver popped open the trunk and got out of the car. He helped load four canvas bags, and got back into the car as the shop owner waited on the walk. As soon as the sedan began to pull away, Derek ran out into the street behind it, narrowly dogging traffic, and shouting into his phone over the din of squealing tires and blaring car horns.

"Jack, are you there? Copy this plate. Now! Get this." Derek ran down the street behind the sedan as it rolled out into traffic. "It's from Jersey, Jack. November Alpha Bravo 87. You got that, Jack? November Alpha Bravo 87!"

"I got it, Derek! I got it. November Alpha Bravo 87."

Derek jumped out of the street, winded and collapsed against a wall to catch his breath. For an instant, he remembered why he had decided to quit smoking. Then he looked up to see the box shop owner heading rapidly toward him along the walk and remembered why he had decided to quit being a P.I.. The man did not look happy.

"I was just leaving." Derek shouted over his shoulder as he dashed off into the night.

Derek ran more than a block before he remembered Jack. He quickly put his phone back up to his ear, panting hard.

"Jack!" he shouted, gasping for air. "Jack, you still there?"

The battery was dead. Damn! Derek decided it was time to head for home.

The Fat Woman

Dear Writetress,

My husband and I have been married for six years. During that time, I've gained about fifty pounds. He recently asked me to lose some weight and I was terribly hurt by his request. He knows that I have tried many times to lose weight, but can't seem to make it happen. Now I am afraid he is going to leave me or cheat on me with someone more attractive. I don't want to lose him. Please tell me what I should do.

Sincerely,

Beatrice Smith

—

Dear Beatrice,

I hear that you are feeling scared, rejected and alone. I also suspect that you want your husband to love you no matter how much you weigh. I can't presume to tell you what is best for you to do, but I can offer some insights that may help you decide for yourself what course of action to take.

Know this: Being overweight is not the issue, it is only the <u>symptom</u> of an issue. There is some aspect of yourself that is serving you well by causing you to weigh more than you'd like. Your true task is not to release the weight, but to discover what purpose it serves for you, acknowledge the weight for serving that purpose, and to lovingly release that purpose from your life forever. Once you accomplish that, the extra weight no longer has a reason to stay. It would be my guess that you will find it falling away with more grace and ease than you could ever have imagined. Without releasing the underlying purpose for being overweight, the weight itself may be released temporarily, but will most likely return in service again, until its reason for being is resolved.

Begin by examining the aspect of yourself that is comfortable with your present size. How does the weight serve you? Is it a means of protection from intimacy? Is it a fear of lack? A wish to become 'invisible?' Or something else entirely? Only you can answer this question for yourself, but once you do, you will be in a better position to choose whether or not you want to face the issue, heal it and release the weight once and for all.

Be kind to yourself in the process of your Self-exploration. Though it is traditional in our society to berate ourselves for our perceived shortcomings - guilt, criticism, manipulation and shame are not effective healing agents of long-term change, and they never have been. Remember to forgive any harsh judgments you may have made about yourself or your weight. Show acknowledgement, gratitude and appreciation for whatever service the extra weight has provided in your life. If losing weight is pursued with loving compassion toward yourself, you may find that the weight releases naturally as you become more attentive to the health of your precious physical body.

Please love yourself, Beatrice. Love yourself always. Love yourself no matter what your husband or mother or neighbor or anyone else says or does or thinks. Accept yourself as you are, right now and today. Love that Self with all your heart and see where that takes you.

Express boundless gratitude for your strong and healthy body that can speak and hear and touch and taste and walk and talk and work and carry things — because not everyone's can. Love yourself so much that your love grows even bigger than your beautiful body and spills out onto everyone and everything around you. You are deserving and you are worth it.

Your physical body may not be perfect in your eyes, and your actions may not always be what you want them to be, but love yourself anyway. You are quite simply a perfect soul having a perfectly imperfect, human experience. We all are. Your true essence is one of divine perfection. Your human experience will be filled with all the situations you need to help you learn whatever it is you've come here to learn. See yourself as perfect, accept your human experience, and forgive and love yourself and your husband. If you lose weight, fine. If not, fine. It doesn't change what you truly are inside — which is strong and ideal and divine.

I do hope this letter brings you peace. I suspect it is not the type of answer you were hoping for, but it is the truth as I know it to be. Having read your letter, I feel a great deal of love for you. I will remember you in my meditations where I shall always see you as whole and complete, just as you already are.

Please remember to:

Acknowledge what is,

Accept what is,

And respond to what is, with love.

Yours in the light,

W.

The Angry Man

Dear Writetress,

Your sugar-coated theories all sound really nice, and I'm sure they appeal to people who don't like to think too hard and like to look at everything through rose colored glasses. But you have completely overlooked the fact that the real world is filled with evil and evil has to be stamped out. If the rest of us just sat around and "accepted" monsters like Hitler, lovey-dovey preachers like you wouldn't even be alive to spout your silly feel-good nonsense. <u>Some people</u> don't get to be all namby-pamby for a living and <u>some people</u> are actually taking charge and making a difference in the world instead of just telling people to "accept what is." Grow up and get real, would you? People like you are doing more harm than good by teaching other people to deny reality.

Gabriel Weston

—

Dear Gabriel,

I appreciate your having taken the time to share your thoughts with me. You raise some good points in your letter, and I assure you that I do take them very seriously. I hear you saying that if everyone were to simply "accept what is," then people would be in danger of overlooking the negative and evil things happening around them, and that the civilized world may very well decay completely while we sit there and just "accept" it.

If I understand your point of view correctly, then I have not been clear in my use of the phrase "to accept what is," and I would like to clarify that for both of us now.

Many people spend vast amounts of energy failing to accept what is. They judge what is, they spend countless hours talking about how things "should" be different, they fail to achieve the things they want to in life because of "the way things are" for them. "If only things were different," they sigh, and continue to spend their lives in ways that they do not find satisfying, and then one day, they die.

I can't count the number of times that people have said to me, "If only I had gone to college, I could have made something of myself." "If only my mother had treated me better, I wouldn't be such a screw-up today." "If only I hadn't married so young, I could have been more successful." "If only I weren't so old/young/disabled/you-fill-in-the-blank." The list is endless.

To accept what is, means to take personal responsibility for what is happening in your life right now. It means not blaming your mother, your father or circumstance for what you are choosing, at this moment, to be. So what if you didn't go to college? Make something of yourself anyway. So what if your mother wasn't perfect? You're responsible for yourself now. So what if circumstances aren't what you'd like them to be? Change them to suit your current ideas of what you want your life to look like.

So that's what I'm teaching, Gabriel. Not that people are to sit back and acquiesce while others around them are being unjustly treated — but that they must fully accept their role in co-creating and shaping their own reality here on this earth — and that they can only truly do it from a place of love that comes from within — not from a place of hatred, anger, judgment or fear.

By the way, your letter demonstrates another form of "denying reality" that is widely accepted and dangerously prevalent in the thinking of many people today. While it is fashionable to refer to people who do things that we judge as evil as "monsters" or "terrorists" or some other loathsome title, that is simply a form of denial designed to make ourselves feel better — and not expressive of reality at all. Adolph Hitler was not a "monster," he was a human being just like we all are. People who hijack airplanes, kidnap children, rape, kill, and steal are not members of some other species that we could not possibly understand. They are having a human experience, just as we all are. They have simply chosen to nurture and feed their anger and their hate and their fear, instead of their loving. There is not one among us who is not capable of harming others if we choose to feed our fears, fuel our angry aspects, or honor our hatred. Living in the light and adding love to the world, is an active, responsible and ongoing choice; and it is the choice I am advocating as loudly as possible, as a preferable way for all people to live.

Adolph Hitler did not act alone. There were hundreds of thousands of people only too willing to yield to their own shadow sides and do harm to others on his behalf. If his countrymen had been anchored in love for their fellow human beings, instead of acting from their fears and prejudices, Hitler's words would have fallen upon deaf ears, and you and I would never have heard his name. That is why it is so urgent for each and every one of us to do our own inner work, find the place inside ourselves where love lives, and then to feed it with all we've got. It's our duty to the world to be the most loving, forgiving, generous, grateful and centered people we can possibly be, and to help others do the same.

Until such time when all people of the world realize that they are one, you are right in thinking that there will be those sent to "stamp out" certain behaviors. I understand the present earthly reality of *wars and soldiers and deadly disputes all too well. My only prayer is that each soldier being sent into battle will go in, not as a frightened, hateful, vengeful killer capable of slaughtering innocents identified only as faceless "enemies," but as a noble warrior, anchored in his own loving center, in touch with true guidance from above, and able to pursue the goals of his army with the knowing ability to discern "the highest good of all concerned" in each passing moment. It is my highest hope that in the "stamping out" of "monsters" that honorable men and women do not become monsters themselves.*

I hope my words have clarified my deeper meaning for you, Gabriel. Again, I thank you for writing to me and I will hold you always in the light.

   Please remember to:
Acknowledge what is,
   Accept what is,
      And respond to what is, with love.
Yours in the light,
W.

As she sealed the orange envelope that held her reply to Gabriel, Anika sighed deeply. There was so much hatred and anger in the world that at times, it felt insurmountable. On days like today, love seemed an insubstantial weapon in the war of energies, but it was all she had.

Anika took hold of a smooth, ivory sheet and without really thinking about it, began to write.

—

Hi Kitten,
I just wanted you to know how glad I am that you're in the world. You are a shining beacon of love and light. I'm sorry you

haven't been able to visit yet, but I understand that your job keeps you busy. They're so lucky to have you.

Do you remember my publisher, Tom? You met him once when you were little. Anyway, he sent me a flattering article from the Times. Those reporters are certainly relentless. I guess I knew they'd come looking for me sooner or later. Well, they haven't found me yet! With luck, by the time they knock on my door, I will have actually become the enlightened guru-type they're seeking. Keep your fingers crossed for me.

I love you.
Mom

The Seeker VII

J ack was already in the office when Derek let himself in the next morning. He was sitting on the floor in the corner, surrounded by the once neat pile of Writetress books, flipping through one entitled, *Light Centered Living.* Derek was surprised to see him.

"What are you doing here?"

"I'm working. With you. On this case." Jack said firmly.

"But . . ." Derek started to protest but Jack cut him off.

"No buts! And you don't have to tell me anything about the client, okay?"

Derek nodded, lips pursed, considering. "Maybe. . ." he said.

"Look, I just need two more supervised months to get my license, and besides, you need help. This is one huge mother of a case. And a really cool one too. So here I am, at your service." Jack concluded.

Derek looked doubtful.

"And for slave wages." Jack added.

Derek thought for a second and nodded. Jack was right. This was one huge mother of a case and he wasn't really enjoying it anyway. For some strange reason, Jack actually *wanted* to be a gumshoe. It would be a relief for Derek when he could turn the entire agency over to his friend and quit the business altogether. "Okay, whaddya got for me?" he asked.

"I had Eddie down at the station run a make on the plate. It's owned by a company out of Union City called Starburst Messenger service. I checked 'em out. They have three offices: the one here in Jersey, Evergreen, Colorado; and Marina Del Rey, California."

"Marina Del Rey?" Derek repeated.

"Yep. And get this, their number is unlisted! What kind of messenger business has an unlisted number?"

Derek furrowed his brow and blinked. This was gonna take a smoke. He reached for a cigarette.

"So, I did a little more checking," Jack continued, "and the entire company has only been in business for eight months! That means they started up right before The Writetress . . . er, I mean Ms Lucio, disappeared, right?"

"Yeah."

"So, I think," Jack said, "that your missing person has purchased her very own messenger company!"

Derek struggled to put it all together.

"What gets me is why?" Jack continued. "Why would anyone want to rent an entire mailbox place when they could just rent one mailbox? And why own their own messenger company when they could just hire an existing one?"

"Privacy," Derek said.

"Privacy?"

"Extreme privacy. Having one dedicated customer means the business only needs one employee, or in the case of the messenger company, two or three employees max. Less likelihood of someone spilling the beans – especially if it means they would lose their livelihood." Derek shook his head in admiration for Anika's system.

"In effect, all these people are on her staff, and some of them probably don't even know it!" he continued. "I bet only one person in the whole chain really knows where she is, and everyone else just passes things along."

"That's gotta cost a fortune," Jack said.

"Well, that's exactly what she's got," Derek sighed. "Anything worth looking at in those books?" He gestured to the pile of Writetress books Jack had been reading.

"Oh yeah" Jack replied a bit too enthusiastically for Derek's taste. "They're great. Amazing, actually. You know what it says here?"

"I have no idea."

"Oh man, you should read these. They're so great. She says everything boils down to love. Love! Isn't that something?"

"You're scaring me, Jack," Derek said.

"Well, I guess you gotta read it for yourself." Jack put the book down, a little embarrassed. "It doesn't sound right when I say it out of context."

Derek tried not to roll his eyes too obviously.

"Anyway, it's a good thing I took a look," Jack said as he began rebuilding the pile of books. "I noticed her publisher is Whitmark. I know a girl who works there."

"Really? Now *that's* interesting," Derek said. "She's not one of those girls who hates you, is she?"

"No, nothing like that," Jack said. "She's a friend of my niece's at Columbia. I took 'em both to a show for my niece's birthday last month. She's just an intern there or something."

"Can she hook me up with Lucio's publisher or editor or whatever they call it? Maybe he can tell me something he hasn't told everyone else already."

"Probably – I think he's her grandpa or something. I'll give her a call," said Jack. "Hey, you want me to drive out to Union City to check on this messenger service?"

"No," said Derek, lighting up another cigarette. "I want you to go to Marina Del Rey."

"Really? You want me to go to California? For real?"

"Yeah, there's a P.I. out there getting info from one of my sources and I need to know more about why he's looking for the same person I'm looking for."

"Think your client is hedging his bets?"

"That's what I want you to find out. I'll hook you up with the source. She thinks I'm a reporter looking to do a story on Ms Writetress and she's eager to help."

"Great. I'm on it! Wow! I gotta go pack. I've never actually been out there before."

"Oh, you'll fit right in. Big Writetress fans, those Angelinos."

"Okay. Here I go. I'll let you know what I find out."

"Take those with you if you like 'em so much," Derek gestured to the pile of books.

"Really? Sure!" Jack was suddenly self-conscious. "I mean, I'll just take a couple here. For now. You know. Gotta travel light. Right?" He hastily grabbed a handful of The Writetress books without looking up at Derek. He was almost out the door when he paused. "Hey. You gonna be okay while I'm gone?"

"What's that supposed to mean?"

"Well, just that, you know, you only have three more days in your apartment. I might not be back by then."

"Oh, yeah. Okay. Uh . . . "

"You want a key to my place?" Jack asked.

Derek nodded. "Yeah, I guess I do. Thanks."

"No problem. Sorry I won't be here to help you move in. But hey! Maybe we can find her before then, huh?"

Derek knew false bravado when he heard it, but he appreciated it nonetheless.

"You're a good pal, Jack," he said.

Jack was halfway down the hall when Derek called after him. "Hey! You might as well give me all your smokes before you go. California is a non-smoking state."

Jack came back, wide-eyed. "For real?" he asked.

Derek smiled. Jack could be so gullible sometimes. "Pretty much. No smoking in restaurants, buildings, bars, anywhere people breathe, basically. It's pure hell, I'm telling you."

"Well, I'll be dammed." Jack dug in his shirt pocket for a mangled pack. He tossed it onto the desk in front of Derek. "Good thing I only smoke when you're around, huh? Just to make you more comfortable, you know?" At that he headed out of the office on his way to California, leaving Derek behind watching with narrowed eyes and wondering who was really the gullible one.

The Addict

Dear Writetress,

I'm at rock bottom and I got nowhere else to turn. I am writing to you from a shelter where they say I can get mail, only I don't get no mail. I got nobody and nothing in my life and it's my own damn fault. No one gives a shit about me and I'm not even sure I give a shit for myself. A lady here said I should write to you because I used to like your books back when I had a house and a family and a car and a job. But that was a long time ago, I think. At least you're someone real to talk to.

I hate to tell you, but I'm a stinking drunk. I don't just drink beer either. I drink anything I can get my hands on and I don't care how I get it. Sometimes I wake up in the morning and I don't even remember how I got to where I am. I don't remember too good.

Don't tell me to stop drinking 'cause I can't. I used to have everything and now all I want is another drink and maybe some mail is all.

Yours truly,
George Berry

—

Dear George,

It was good to hear from you. Thank you for writing to me. It sounds like things are tough for you right now, but maybe all you need is a small spot of hope. I'm not sure I'm the one to offer it up, but please allow me to try. After all, when one is at "rock bottom" there is only one direction to go, right?

You may feel bad about yourself and your situation, but I want you to know some things that are absolutely true about you. For one thing, you are a precious child of God with an inner essence that is divine and holy and perfect just as it is. Your human experience may currently be a challenging one, but I know and trust that all is well at the level of your higher self. At that level of your being, you are pure love and light and wisdom. The aspect of yourself that is addicted to alcohol is simply the human experience that your perfect soul is having at this brief moment in time.

So, stay drunk if you want to, George! You have my permission. It really is okay. If you want to be a drunk, then be a drunk and be a damn good one. Accept it, embrace it and drink with gusto and joy. If, one day, you come to want something different out of life, something more perhaps, please trust that you are free and capable enough to choose that too. Many fine avenues of help await, only for you to do the asking.

It has been written that, "not one soul will be lost," and that most certainly includes yours. We are all on our way home and none of us can judge our own path or that of another. I for one, trust that your current human experience is unfolding exactly as it needs to for your highest good. Remember that earth is a school and this life is your curriculum. It doesn't matter what "classes" you choose because at some point, we all graduate. There are no mistakes. You can't get it wrong. We're all just learning. All of us. You are and always will be a divine and deserving being. Be what you need to be now and in time you will come more and more into alignment with that place inside of you that knows your true essence.

Forgive yourself, George, and love yourself as I love you. I will remember you always in my meditations where I will see you as you truly are: whole, perfect and divine.

Please remember to:

Acknowledge what is,

Accept what is,

And respond to what is, with love.

Yours in the light,

W.

The Seeker VIII

It was dark when Derek let himself into the apartment, ignoring the eviction notice pasted on the door. The light on his landline answering machine was blinking. There was only one person who still used that number. He sighed heavily and decided to listen to the message anyway.

"Derek it's me," came the familiar, now grating tone. "You know what your problem is? Your problem is you got no ambition. You're never gonna amount to anything! That's your problem. And I just want you to know it's over between us. You can forget about coming to get me this time because I ain't coming back no matter what! We're finished. I hope you understand that."

The voice softened before continuing, "I know this is hard for you, Baby, so if you wanna talk about it, I'm at my Mom's. So, you can call me there anytime, okay? But I'm telling you, we're through. I'll be home tonight if you wanna talk. Call me, okay? Bye, bye now, Baby."

Cassandra used to drive Derek crazy, mostly because he suspected she was right about all his inadequacies, but just now he was too tired to care. He put out his cigarette and fell face down on the bed, clothes still on. He was asleep before he could even feel ashamed about not amounting to anything in life.

The Unsure

Dear Writetress,

   I have no idea what to do with my life. I was a gifted student in school and did well in all my studies. I am interested in many things, but not passionate about anything except learning more and more things that I seem to have no real use for. I have been told I am a "Jack of all trades and a Master of none." I should be earning a good living by now, but instead I keep trying different things. I get interested in one thing for a while and then I lose interest and try something else. I have worked for restaurants, banks, department stores, consulting firms, hospitals, schools, television shows, music publishers and more. I don't have any idea what my purpose is in life or what Spirit put me here to do. Please help me figure out what my true-life purpose is.

   Sincerely,
   Dan Evans

—

Dear Dan,

   What an interesting and exciting life you have had! It sounds like you are a man who confidently follows his dreams and you've had a lot of them. How much more wonderful it would be if you were able to accept and be happy with your lifestyle as it is, instead of *judging it as being somehow "wrong" or "bad" simply because of some words that others may have said to you.*

Your natural drive and learning orientation to life is a tremendously positive thing, especially since we are all here on the physical plane to learn and grow and to help each other. Although we all come to this earth school with a "purpose," it has little to do with our occupational choices. We're here to practice and with luck, master spiritual lessons such as compassion, happiness, love, wisdom, kindness, forgiveness, acceptance, sharing, generosity, service, oneness, and gratitude. Any and all of those lessons can be learned and practiced and mastered in any profession you can name. In fact, simply living on earth, gives us ample opportunities to practice our lessons, whether in the context of a profession or not.

I urge you to consider each circumstance you find yourself in, each encounter you may have with another precious being, as an opportunity for your own spiritual growth. What you're doing, where you are, or what people think of you has no bearing on your earthly training. All that matters is how you comport yourself, both inside and out, while you're here. Learn to unconditionally love and accept and forgive yourself and you'll soon find yourself able to love and accept and forgive others. Sell shoes while you do it or heal the sick or sign autographs for your fans. It just doesn't matter.

Work is nothing more than a spiritual laboratory — a place to rehearse and practice and try to be centered in our loving awareness again and again and again until we get it right. There are no mistakes and there are no failures. We're all in school and we're all just learning. So you see, Dan? Your love of learning can and will indeed serve you well. Next lessons for you? How about self-acceptance and trust and love and forgiveness? Ready? Go ahead and get started. I'm excited for you.

Please remember to:
Acknowledge what is,
Accept what is,
And respond to what is, with love.
Yours in the light,
W.

—

Hi Honey,

Tom has been keeping me abreast of the growing media search for my whereabouts. I never realized it would become such an exciting game of cat and mouse for them. I might have known something was up when I received twice as much mail as usual this week. Well, I suppose it's worth appreciating if it means there's nothing more urgent going on for them to write about. I do hope they're not disappointed with whatever results they eventually achieve.

I hope you and André are doing well. I miss you desperately and look forward to the day when you can come for a nice long visit.

I love you forever,
Mom

The Wood Man II

In the spring and summer, when the weather was mild, Danny brought wood for Anika's fire twice a month. Now that Autumn was in full color, he came twice every week, in order to adequately bolster her supply for the rapidly approaching winter months.

Today the porch already held as many logs as it could accommodate and Danny was going to begin a new pile, under the lean-to alongside the cabin, around the corner from where Anika sat writing in her rocker. She wouldn't be able to watch him work from her usual vantage point, and noted her sadness with some surprise and curiosity.

Why don't I just get up and move? she wondered as she heard Danny's pickup pull into the drive.

Although she didn't really know the answer, Anika stayed put as the truck disappeared around the corner. She could hear him stacking the logs beside the cabin as meticulously as he had those on the porch. She tried to focus on the letter she was holding, but her own uneasiness surprised her. It was difficult to concentrate. She had just about decided to give up and go watch Danny, when a letter she had opened absent-mindedly caught her attention. Neatly typed on a small, folded piece of stationery, it read:

```
Dear Writetress,
   How do you know that the things you are saying
   are true?
Sincerely,
Helen Parker
```

Anika was a bit taken aback and wondered how in the world she could ever answer Helen's reasonable but somehow annoying query. She could write about the differences between belief and direct knowing or the subjective nature of truth. She could talk about her years of spiritual studies, or she could point to the mass popularity of her books. *Sixty million people can't be wrong*, she thought, knowing that the idea was false even before the instant rebuttal echoed in her mind, *Oh yes they can!*

Anika didn't know how long she had been lost in thoughts of possible answers to Helen, when something caught the corner of her eye and startled her. She looked up and saw Danny standing quite nearby with his usual armload of wood. He was looking at her in a way she had never seen before and she wondered how long he had been silently observing her. She gathered her wits and smiled up at him. He beckoned her with a nod of his head. She absentmindedly stuffed Helen's note into the pocket of her jacket and got up to hold the front door open for her wood man.

Once inside they moved in opposite directions; Danny to the hearth with his wood and Anika to the refrigerator on a quest for the lemonade she had made fresh for him this morning. For the first time ever, and out of pure anxiety, Anika addressed Danny as he sipped his drink.

"You probably think I'm an old fool," she said, "just sitting out there muttering to myself."

Anika waited but there was no reply. Danny just smiled kindly and continued to sip his lemonade. He appeared to be listening, however, so Anika continued.

"I just got a letter I don't know how to answer, you know?" Danny remained attentive but still. He seemed interested enough. His steady, wheezing breath provided a welcome accompaniment for Anika's voice and somehow urged her to go on with her story.

"I feel I owe this woman an answer to her question, but I don't know the best way to explain. It's complicated."

Danny said nothing, but something in the nature of his attentiveness encouraged Anika to continue. It had been a while since she'd had someone to talk to, and now, in her agitated state, she couldn't seem to stop herself.

"I came up here because people were starting to say things about me that weren't true, you know?"

The question was rhetorical and Danny seemed to know it. He didn't interrupt.

"There was this reporter who wrote an article about me in a major newspaper. He said that when I entered the room for our interview, a longstanding medical condition of his was instantly healed! All I did was walk into the room!"

Danny didn't look surprised, or upset or anything at all. But he did look like he was listening.

"People believed him," she continued. "They began showing-up in droves outside my publisher's building. Then they started saying I could walk on water, make food appear on the table out of nowhere, move objects with my mind, and do all manner of other crazy, magical things. They started treating me like I was somehow different than they were – and as soon as people do that – you can't teach them a thing. They suddenly think that the things you know couldn't possibly apply to them and their normal, everyday, run-of-the-mill lives."

Anika thought she perceived a slight nod from Danny, as though he understood all too well what she was talking about. Or maybe it was just her imagination.

"People love to think that those who are "spiritual" are somehow "different." It relieves them of the responsibility of growing spiritually in the here-and-now of their own lives," Anika sighed before continuing.

"The problem is, people don't like someone to be too different. That eventually scares them. And it scared me! I knew I couldn't be what they thought I already was. So, I ran away."

Danny continued to listen attentively, his expression one of near adoration, his lemonade glass long empty.

"People expected me to do some amazing things that I have no idea how to do. And you know what the worst part is?"

Danny waited to hear.

"I started to believe them. I thought there was something wrong with me because I hadn't mastered the party tricks and parlor games of the spiritually enlightened. I felt I had to perform acts of spiritual showmanship just to be a valid spiritual writer. I began to feel like an imposter."

Anika felt another wave of tears and knew she should stop burdening this simple country boy with issues he couldn't possibly understand or relate to. But still, he did seem interested, even though he said nothing. Maybe he couldn't speak.

"Anyway," she concluded, "that's why I'm here today. I figured if I came up here and spent some time with myself and Spirit, that maybe I really could become all those things they expected of me. But sooner or later they're going to find me and I'm afraid they're going to be very disappointed."

She blew her nose and moved toward the door, letting Danny know that she was done talking and he was free to go.

"I am glad to be here though," she almost sounded convinced, "because I would never have met you otherwise. Thanks for listening."

Danny smiled, but instead of passing directly through the door, he moved over to Anika and grabbed her up into the warmest and most sincere hug she could ever remember getting from anyone. At first, she stiffened in surprise, but as she let herself relax into the softness of the embrace, Anika felt yet another surge of tears. Even though Danny may not have understood her words, he somehow understood that she really needed a hug.

After what seemed like a long time, Danny released his grip on Anika, smiled up at her, and headed around the side of the house, back to his now empty truck. Anika returned to her rocker and sighed. What a beautiful person her friend Danny was.

As she settled back into her seat, Helen Parker's letter instantly tugged at Anika's awareness again. How *did* she know that the things she said were true? How indeed? She was certainly confident in her beliefs, and had trained for many years to acquire them, but how could she express the reasons behind her confidence?

As she mused, Anika heard a noise and looked up. Danny's truck was now alongside the porch. It stopped and he rolled down the window, looking at her expectantly. She smiled at him.

"Just tell her you don't know," he said.

The words were slurred and a bit stilted, but unmistakable in their meaning. Danny grinned at Anika's dropped jaw before he waved and drove off. Anika stared after him for a long time before she remembered to close her mouth.

—

Hello Sweetheart,

I am taking a break. Since I (temporarily) do not know what to write to my readers, I will happily write to you instead! I miss you so much. Funny — when you were growing up, I was so busy being a celebrity and giving my time to the world that I didn't have much time for you. Now that the tables have turned, I realize how painful that must have been. I hope you can forgive me for any hurt you may have felt.

Speaking of giving-up the celebrity lifestyle, I have concluded that housework is highly overrated. I miss my housekeeper almost as much as I miss you. What do you think? Doesn't it seem that someone as "holy" and "spiritual" as I am would be able to handle a little housework with grace and ease? Sigh. How I wish the word "should" had never been created. Now I'll have to stop writing. I'm sure something in the cabin needs dusting. Write me.

I adore you more than you'll ever know.

Love,

Mom

The Writer

Dear Writetress,

I love your books. I wish I could be a successful writer like you, but I can't seem to get the discipline down. My writing teachers say I should write every day if I want to be a real writer. My problem is that I don't write every day. I try, but some days I am too tired or too busy or just not in the mood. I love to write, but my teachers say I'm just too lazy to be a real writer. Please tell me how to get the discipline I need to succeed at writing because it's what I really want to do.

Thank you,

Gwen Kim

—

Dear Gwen,

Thank you for writing. How wonderful it is for me to get a letter from a fellow writer! We wordsmiths have to stick together.

Discipline is an interesting concept. If we define it as forcing ourselves to do something we don't really want to do in the moment, just because we think we should — it can be quite unpleasant and difficult to stick to. It's even harder to continue on a disciplined path if we beat ourselves up for not doing it "right" in the first place. But if we view discipline as a loving action, taken by ourSelves, for ourSelves, in our own best interests, because it will lead us to the fulfillment of our heartfelt desires, it suddenly becomes a concept worth considering.

Because you have asked, I will share with you the two biggest secrets of my writing career (and of life in general). Are you ready? Here is the first: Don't "should" on yourself!

There will always be people who are happy to tell you what you should or shouldn't do. "You should write every day," they'll say, or "make sure to write 10 hours a week." I have written dozens of books and I say, poppycock! There is no one way to do <u>anything</u> that works for everyone. Your process is as unique to you as mine is to me, just as your words and your stories will be unique when you get them on the page.

So, honor yourself and your own creative process. Find out what works best for <u>you</u> and stick with it. Love it and cherish it and protect it from anyone who thinks they know better. If you write a page a day, you'll write more words than if you write a page a week or a page a month or a page a year. If you write more words, you'll learn more about your own unique style of writing sooner rather than later. Is writing the words faster or more copiously; "better?" No. Does writing more often help you fall in love with your own work? I believe it does.

That brings me to secret number two: Be kind to yourself while you write. Learn to appreciate the process for what it is. It is more important to love your process than to judge your results. The reason it is more important is because writing is a practice — just like life itself. That's really what writing (or any other profession) is — a reflection of life. If you're hard on yourself in life, you'll be hard on yourself as you write, and you'll probably be hard on other people too. If you're kind to yourself when you write, you'll find that practice of kindness rubbing off in other areas of life as well — and you may even find that you enjoy writing more often, without resorting to a harsh and self-abusing form of discipline. Sometimes other people will like what you write and sometimes they won't. It doesn't matter whether they do or not — as long as you are kind to yourself while writing it.

I look forward to reading your work one day.

Please remember to:

Acknowledge what is,

Accept what is,

And respond to what is, with love.

Yours in the light,

W.

The Writetress smiled to herself as she reread her reply to Gwen. The messages about not "shoulding" on ourselves and enjoying the process of the work seemed written by another hand. She laughed aloud when she thought of what she herself had written to Corinne just the night before, regarding her own feelings about life without a housekeeper.

As she sealed the pink envelope that seemed to match Gwen's energy most aptly, Anika's eyes fell upon a straw broom leaning against the porch rail. She was puzzled for a moment, and didn't remember seeing it there before. She concluded that Danny must have left it out the last time he made a delivery. But that wasn't like him at all. He must be trying to tell her something. Anika smiled as she picked up the broom and began slowly and mindfully sweeping the front porch, in deep appreciation for mountain dust, golden aspen leaves, gusts of wind, and her wondrous friend Danny.

The Seeker IX

"I'm afraid I'm not likely to be of much help," said Tom Miller, Anika's publisher, as he showed Derek into his paper-strewn office. "But my granddaughter asked very nicely if I would meet with you," he chuckled. "She even said, "please," bless her heart. Apparently, your friend Jack made quite an impression on her."

Derek looked around the cozy office. Hundreds of hopeful manuscripts in various stages of non-publication were piled everywhere, even on the chairs. The walls were covered with an assortment of framed awards that Derek suspected were rather difficult to win.

"I really appreciate your time," Derek said as Tom politely freed a chair for him from underneath a stack of tattered manuscripts.

The look of the place surprised Derek. He had expected something more like a penthouse suite. Tom Miller was, after all, the publisher of the biggest literary sensation going, and a well-known philanthropist to boot. He was known for contributing generously to literacy efforts around the world. The one office concession to his greatness was a generous window overlooking most of Manhattan. Derek got the feeling that Tom often stood by that window and gazed out over the city, probably lost in thought.

"I'm looking for Anika Lucio," Derek said as he sat down.

"You and everyone else," Tom chuckled as he seated himself behind his desk. "You're not the only private eye I'll speak with today. See this stack of messages?" He gestured to a pile of pink, phone message paper on his desk. The pile was three inches high. "These are just from this morning. Reporters, detectives, old school chums, everyone seems to think I know where she is."

"Don't you?"

"No. Of course not. I don't think anyone does."

"But how can that be? How can someone so well-known just disappear like that?"

"Ah! That is the question, isn't it young man?" Tom leaned way back in his chair and laced his fingers across his chest as he stared at something on the ceiling that Derek couldn't see. "Anika Lucio is not just "someone" as you call her. She is a very special someone, who has ways of getting just about anything she wants. And right now, she wants to be alone."

"What makes her so special?" Derek asked.

Tom's eyebrows shot up at the question. He regarded Derek intently for a moment before responding with a question of his own. "Have you read any of her books?"

"Well, no. Not exactly." Derek stammered. "I've been meaning to."

"I think you'll find the answer to your question there. Ani is quite unlike anyone I've ever had the pleasure of knowing. She is blown by breezes most of us don't even feel, and I cherish that about her. She's very special."

"What? Is she psychic or something?"

Tom laughed, "Let's just call it 'marvelously attuned,' or 'extraordinarily intuitive,' or 'profoundly authentic,' shall we?"

"Do you have any idea where she might be hiding?"

"Nope. Not a clue."

"But I read that you've been in touch with her since her disappearance," Derek said.

"Oh, I drop her a note from time to time. Sometimes she even responds, but not often."

Derek sighed in frustration. "Do you know anything about her family? She has a daughter, right?"

"Ah, you know about Corinne?" Tom seemed impressed. "Most people don't know about her. Ani has done a very good job of protecting her from the press."

"Maybe Corinne knows where her mother is," Derek prompted.

"Maybe, but I doubt it," Tom said. "She and Ani haven't spoken for several years. Corinne hates the spotlight and there's nothing but spotlight where Ani is concerned."

"So, you're not in touch with her either?"

"With Corinne?" Tom looked surprised at the question. "I haven't seen Corinne since she was about ten, I think. She's all grown up now."

"What about the girl's father? Is he in the picture?" Derek asked even though he already knew the answer.

"Ani's husband died in the war when Corinne was just a little girl. It happened long before Ani became The Writetress and many years before I even met her. She never remarried."

Derek was frustrated. This was going nowhere. A thought occurred to him, "What's all this stuff I keep hearing about her eyes?" he asked.

"Ah! You've heard about Ani's eyes." Tom smiled thoughtfully to himself and got up from behind his desk. He walked over to the window and looked out with a reflective gaze, just as Derek had pictured him. He was quiet for a long time.

"Her eyes are very precious." He said quietly. "Very precious indeed."

Derek leaned forward to better hear the old man. "Did you say, precious?" he asked.

Tom took a deep breath and came back from wherever it was he had gone. "I did say precious," he said nodding.

"I've heard they can heal the sick or freak people out or all kinds of strange things. You're not sitting here telling me that one look into her eyes can really do all that, are you?"

Tom regarded Derek kindly for what felt like a long time. Derek squirmed under the old man's gaze.

"It's just love," Tom said after a time.

"Love?"

"Pure, unadulterated, unconditional love," Tom affirmed. "Never seen anything quite like it. Don't expect I ever will."

"Are you saying she just *loves* people and they think something incredible has happened to them?"

"Well, love is pretty incredible, wouldn't you say?" Tom began moving toward the door, signaling an impending end to the conversation. "I'd venture to guess few people on earth have known complete and utter love like that, even for a few seconds. Everyone reacts differently of course, but make no mistake about it, it's love, pure and simple that comes out of those eyes of hers."

Derek rose, stunned by what he had just heard. He had almost glided out of the office completely lost in thought before he remembered that this was his last chance to get something that might point to where Anika Lucio was.

"Just tell me where you send your mail to her. I know you don't use the main address like the general public. Please? Just the zip code?" he begged as the two men entered the elevator lobby.

Tom laughed and shook his head. "You certainly are tenacious. I like that. Sorry, but it's a local address. I'm sure it gets forwarded at least a half dozen times by as many people before it gets to wherever it's going. Unless of course, she's hiding right here under our noses." Tom shrugged with a smile and shook Derek's hand. "Good luck, son. Read one of Ani's books. I trust you'll enjoy it. You're a fine young man. I hope whatever you're doing is ultimately worth it to you."

He hopes that whatever I'm doing is worth it to me? What's that supposed to mean? Derek's thoughts spun with the old man's words as the elevator door closed on his best lead. His head whirled, he wanted a cigarette badly, his partner had been in California for two days, he had to vacate his apartment by tomorrow morning, and he was no closer to finding Anika Lucio. Things just kept getting better and better and better.

* * *

Derek let himself into the dark apartment, ignoring the swastika someone had drawn on the eviction notice. The light on his answering machine was blinking like crazy. He sighed heavily, yanked the machine out of the wall and tossed it into a box. He wasn't really in the mood to hear Cassandra point out what his problems were at the moment.

For the next two hours, everything that would fit into a box got thrown into one. Things that didn't fit got piled by the door. He was surprised and disgusted by the amount of stuff he owned. In the morning, he'd probably leave most of it behind anyway. Like everything else in his life, it was just more junk that didn't seem to matter anymore.

Just as Derek sealed the last box, his cell phone rang. He fumbled around through one of the piles and found it by the third ring.

"Derek! It's me! Jack!"

"Hey! Jack!"

"I'm out here in California."

"Yeah, that was the plan. How's it going out there?"

"Great! Just great!" Jack already sounded annoyingly Angelinoesque. "It's like summer out here! Can you beat that? Summer on the last day of September!"

"Jack, what about the case? Did you find anything out about this Paul guy?"

"Oh, yeah. Well no. Not yet. Sandy has been just showing me around, you know, but Paul hasn't called or nothing."

"Sandy has been showing you around?" Derek was incredulous.

"Yeah, just, you know, helping me get oriented. She's letting me stay at her place too. Real nice gal, Sandy." Jack's voice lowered to a whisper, "And Derek, guess what?"

"What?"

"She's a total babe. I mean hot in that California kind of way! And I think she likes me!"

This was more than Derek could take right now. "Jesus, Jack! I send you out there to work on a case and you start making moves on my source?"

Jack was hurt. "I thought you'd be happy for me, Boss."

"I am happy for you. I mean, no! I'm not! My life is falling apart while you're out in California having a great time on a case that's destroying me, and I'm supposed to be happy for you? And don't call me Boss!"

"Okay, Boss, uh, I mean, Derek."

"Shit, Jack. Have you found out even one thing on this case in the last two days? Even one?"

"Well yeah, that's why I was calling actually." Jack said. "Sandy and me, we drove to the Marina today to check out the address of that Starburst messenger service here, and guess what?"

"Mail drop?"

"Yeah!" Jack was impressed. "How'd you know?"

"Because I went by the one in Jersey today. Same thing. There's no there, there."

"Guess that just leaves Denver, huh?"

"Guess so."

"You want me to check it out?" Jack sounded reluctant.

"No, that's okay. You stay in California for a while and keep your eye on this Paul guy. One of us might as well have some fun. I'll go check out Denver. Got no place to lay my head here anymore anyway."

"Oh man, that's right" Jack remembered, "You're moving into my place tomorrow, huh?"

"Well, I'm moving outta here. Not sure where to yet. I might just store some junk at your place for a while if that's okay."

"Sure, sure it's okay, Derek. Whatever you need."

"I mean, I'll be in Denver for a couple days, then I'll have to figure something out when I get back here."

"Whatever you need, Derek. Su casa es my casa, or whatever the heck they say."

"Thanks, Jack. You're a pal."

Derek hung up the phone and lit a cigarette. He spent the last night in his apartment sitting in the dark, staring out the window at nothing in particular, smoking, and wishing Tom Miller were his father. He fell asleep there, his forehead pressed against the glass and the publisher's words swimming in his dreams: *It's just love. I hope whatever you're doing is ultimately worth it to you. You're a fine young man. It's just love. You're a fine young man. It's just love. It's love.*

The Victim

Dear Writetress,

    I am 33 years old and have been in therapy for years now. My father did awful and unspeakable things to me when I was a young girl. I told my mother, but she didn't believe me. I had to run away from home when I was 15 just to get away from him. I lived on the streets for years before I finally got my act together and finished school. Now I have a good job and a decent place to live, but I cannot trust any man. I hate my father for what he did to me and I hate all men for what they do to women every single day. You are a woman. Please tell me what to do. I don't want to be in therapy forever.

    Sincerely,

    Allie Larsen

—

Dear Allie,

    I can hear the pain and anger in your letter. You are angry at your father for the things he did to you. You may even be feeling some shame about those things. You feel hurt and betrayed by your mother who didn't believe you when you told her the truth. You had some hard times on the streets and may have had to do some things that you didn't want to do, in order to survive out there. Your first 30 or so years have been rough.

I acknowledge you for coming as far as you have. It wasn't easy for you, but you have made a home for yourself and are working hard to support yourself which is tremendous progress from where you once were. I also acknowledge how hard you are working to heal the inner, more emotional places that were so very hurt by your father's actions all those years ago. Those injured aspects are the same ones that are now working hard to protect you from ever being hurt again, by not allowing you to trust or appreciate the gifts that any man may have to offer.

Please know that what I am about to say, is said with a loving heart and the greatest concern for you that I can possibly muster.

You must let it go!

In order for things to get better for you, you must forgive any judgments that you have placed against your father for what he did. You must forgive your judgments against your mother. You must forgive yourself for any judgments of shame or anger or misbehavior you may have placed on yourself. Anger and hatred and withholding can never heal our wounds — only love can do that. Please apply it liberally to the places inside of you that still hurt.

This isn't about whether your father and mother were right or wrong in what they did to you years ago — this is about the quality of your life from this day forward. What happened in the past happened. There's nothing any of us can do to change it. What you do now, in this moment, is what will determine the kind of life you have tomorrow and in all the days that follow. If you choose not to forgive, if you don't let it go, if you cling to the notion that you are a victim and continue to wear the label voluntarily from this day forward — this is as good as life is going to get for you.

On the other hand, if you are truly ready to rise as a phoenix from the ashes of your past life, if you're ready to claim whatever lessons your circumstances previously held for you and move on to your next higher level of experience, then it's time to let bygones be bygones, as they say.

I'm not implying that you need to spend time with your mother or father, although you may find yourself wanting to as a part of this process, but you do need to work through and let go of the anger and hate and shame that you're carrying around, or they will define you for as long as you carry them in this life, and perhaps into the next.

All this may be difficult to swallow at this point, but I urge you to consider the exhilarating possibility of redefining yourself in whatever manner you choose. Once you move through the pain, it can be quite a freeing and joyful process to start life anew.

Each of us has many stories to tell in this lifetime. Your "story" up until now has been a painful one, but <u>you</u> are the author of your life story from here on out. When you grow weary of telling your old story and start telling a new one, the new story, and your new life, will become whatever you want them to be. Just imagine the possibilities!

I wish for you only what you wish for yourself at your highest and most divine level. I will remember you in my prayers and meditations.

Please remember to:
Acknowledge what is,
Accept what is,
And respond to what is, with love.
Yours in the light,
W.

The Loser

Dear Writetress,

*   I can't get a break. Things always go wrong for me. Every time I think I've found a great job; it turns out that the job or the boss or the people there really suck. Every time I get into a relationship with a new guy, and I think things are going great, we break up. I buy a lottery ticket every week and I never win. I'm broke, my apartment sucks, my landlord is evil and my car is a piece of junk. I have read all your books and a bunch of others. I do what they say but my life isn't working the way I want it to. What do I have to do to get a break in this lifetime?*

*   Sincerely,*

*   Marge Wilson*

—

Dear Marge,

*   Thank you for writing. I hear that you are frustrated with your life. You believe that you have done the work for spiritual growth described in books by myself and others, yet you do not see the outward manifestations you had hoped for here on the physical plane.*

*   I can't tell you how to win the lottery, but I can tell you this: your outer, earthly experience is simply a reflection of your inner reality — no more and no less. No matter how many books you have read or mantras you have chanted, if you perceive yourself as lacking worth,*

your life will reflect that back to you. If you perceive yourself as someone people leave, then people will leave you. If you hold a view of yourself as not deserving of abundance, the universe will comply with that view as well. This is God's way of giving us what we ask for.

Spirit does not judge our inner reality; it simply allows it to manifest on the physical plane. That is the very heart of the concept of free will. We are free to suffer just as we are free to experience joy. We are free to have wealth and abundance and we are free to reject those possibilities for lessons in lack or scarcity, if that is what we believe will serve us best. Although we are not always free to choose our circumstances, we are always free to choose our response to those circumstances.

Spiritual evolution is far more about how you relate to your conditions than it is about what those conditions are. Are you choosing to approach your life (that is, your curriculum for this human experience you are having) with love, forgiveness and acceptance? Or are you choosing instead to practice judgment of yourself and others, criticism, impatience, shame and anger? How you are inside yourself and with yourself as you're experiencing your life is what ultimately matters.

Continue your efforts toward spiritual evolution, and enjoy the journey. No one said it was going to be easy. It's hard work, but ultimately, it's the only work that matters. We simply can't know why Spirit gives us certain circumstances to deal with, we can only trust and have faith that we are somehow being served by them.

Please remember to:
Acknowledge what is,
  Accept what is,
    And respond to what is, with love.
Yours in the light,
W.

The Seeker X

O n Thursday morning, Derek made three trips by cab between his place and Jack's place, and that was enough. The rest of the stuff could stay behind in his old apartment, a gift to his landlord. *Nobody needs more than three trips worth of junk in their life,* he thought as he inhaled a deep lungful of smoke.

He went to the office, logged on to his computer, and started planning his trip to Denver. If the address of Starburst there was just a front, he would call his client and beg off. That would be it. He couldn't take the case any further. It had been nearly a month, he had no apartment, no girlfriend, and he was no closer to finding Anika Lucio. If some holy-whatever, jillionaire really wanted to hide, she could hide for as long as she wanted to. Derek had to get on with putting his life back together, and he intended to do it in a way that was ultimately worth it to him, whatever the hell that meant. After all, he *was* a fine young man, damnit!

The Bad Seed

That same Thursday morning in early October, The Writetress stepped out onto her porch and realized her aspen grove was naked. It had been coming on for some time, the ground below the slender, white trunks increasingly covered in golden, heart-shaped leaves with each gust of autumn wind. And now today, her trees were noticeably quite bare.

Dear Writetress,

My grown son is not a good person. I don't know why he does the things he does. I am ashamed of him. He is mean and spiteful and angry, arrogant and nasty to me and to other people who he doesn't even know. I am afraid he will end up hurting himself or someone else with his out-of-control temper. He may even end up in jail someday. He yells and tries to scare people into doing the things he wants them to do. He has been divorced twice and his own children do not want to see him. I think that is very sad. I don't know what went wrong with him. I tried to raise him to be a better man than he is. His sister is a beautiful person who is loving and kind, but he acts like an animal. What can I do to help him and his children?

Sincerely,
Jeanne Garcault

—

Dear Jeanne,

Thank you for writing to me. I hear the disappointment and sadness in your words. You are bewildered as to why your son acts the way he does. You are hurt when he treats you badly. It pains you to see your grandchildren grow estranged from their father, who was once your sweet little boy. You wish there was something you could do to change the situation for all concerned. If only things could somehow be different . . .

Each of us comes here with our own individual lessons to be learned and previous obligations to fulfill. You are no more responsible for your son's growth as a spiritual being than he is for yours. You cannot save him from his earthly curriculum. None of us can even know what his curriculum is. We can only have faith that he is living the experience that he most needs to have right now.

We cannot always see the whys and wherefores of a given situation. Sometimes we believe that circumstances "should" be different than they are, but when we hold that belief, we are practicing judgment ourselves. All we can do is to release our judgments daily and trust that Spirit is still in charge. It is important that you know things are unfolding for the highest spiritual good of all concerned.

Do your best to release the judgments you have about this situation. Spend some time forgiving yourself for judging your son as bad, your grandchildren as wounded, and yourself as shamed. Shower yourself, your son and his children with love and light on a daily basis — even if only from afar. Remember the power and value of prayer, and practice it daily. Then spend some joyous time with your grandchildren. It sounds like all of you could use the added pleasure in your lives.

I am sending light to you and your family. I see you especially as a shining beacon of peace and joy to them and to the rest of the world.

Please remember to:
Acknowledge what is,
Accept what is,
And respond to what is, with love.
Yours in the light,
W.

The Seeker XI

Derek was accustomed to cold weather, but that October Friday in Denver was far more brisk than he anticipated. Derek hated being cold. He only tolerated it in New York because it was New York. That was reason enough for anybody. But being cold anywhere else, especially on an increasingly hopeless gig, while Jack was all warm in L.A. and getting cozy with Sandy Sanderson, just plain pissed him off.

Even the idea of the majestic Denver scenery annoyed him. What good were mountains anyway? For one thing, they were cold. For another, all you could really do was look at them for a few minutes, and say "oooh," and "aaahhh," a bunch of times. That was pretty much it. After that they just got in your way if you were trying to go someplace. Derek decided it was a good thing he wasn't planning to go much of anyplace here.

His breath froze in the air as he stepped out of the airport and hailed the next cab in line at the curb. He tossed his duffel into the back seat ahead of him, and gave the driver the address of the local Starburst Messenger Service. Then Derek sat back, cracked the window and lit up a smoke. At least he could relax for a few minutes.

"Hey, do you mind not smoking in here, Buddy?" the cab driver asked.

"Excuse me?"

"Makes the car stink. Customers don't like to ride in a stinky car. Don't smoke in here, okay?"

Derek sighed and carefully stubbed out his cigarette. It dangled impotently from his lips as he pondered the irony of anyone in a town full of gunslingers who pack heat in the supermarket, being worried about the smell of a little smoke. It was going to be another one of those days. His head began to ache from the altitude, the lack of air, the lack of smoke, and the lack of a life.

Whatever. When the cab got to the mail drop, he would simply ask the driver to wait, step outside, have a quick cigarette, and get back in the car. He would call his client, admit he was licked, quit this gig once and for all, stay one night in Denver, and head back to New York to start searching for another apartment and a new job. Who knows? He might even give Cassandra a call. It made him feel a little better to have a plan. So what if the plan sucked? It was a plan. That was the important thing. It was a plan. Derek sighed heavily in the back seat of a non-smoking cab in Denver and tried to be happy about it.

The Bereaved Parent

Dear Writetress,

My daughter has died and I cannot bear the pain. My beautiful, young and loving daughter has died. Please help me to feel better. Please.

I have studied your philosophies about how the universe works, but there is still much I don't understand. If we have all been together for many lifetimes before this one, and if we never truly die but just change form, why does this loss hurt so very badly? Why do we feel grief? Why does God hate me so much that he took my beloved daughter from me? Why?

I truly do want to understand and move toward my own healing and enlightenment, but I have been consumed with nothing but thoughts of my dear daughter who died last year. I still cry every night just to hear her voice one more time. I know she is fine and that we will be together again one day, but all I can feel now is pain and loss. Please help.

Sincerely,
Omar Abdul

The Writetress held Omar's letter gently for a long time before selecting a pale blue sheet of paper and slowly beginning to write.

—

Dearest Omar,

Thank you for writing to me during this tender time in your life. You have experienced a great loss that seems as though it can never be healed. It is difficult to experience so much pain. I acknowledge you for your expressions of sorrow and encourage you to honor your own process and continue feeling your feelings for as long as it takes them to pass. Grief is a natural human reaction to such a devastating loss and it must be acknowledged and honored and fully expressed before it can truly move on.

Because I too have felt the pain of grief, even in the knowing that my loved ones are safe and sound and continue to exist, I have thought about this issue before. I can share my thoughts with you here, but I have no way of knowing whether or not you will be able to take any comfort in them. Please bear with me while I try, in my own awkward way, to explain my views on this subject.

In our human state we are creatures of deep biological instinct, and we have an instinct to live. That may have caused most of us to make the (I believe erroneous) judgment early on that to live is a good thing and that to die — which <u>appears</u> to be the opposite of life — is therefore, a bad thing. So, when someone dies, we are conditioned to respond as though a bad thing has happened.

But knowing these things that I hold to be true has not relieved me of the experience of grief. I too have felt the illusion of loss and separation as though it were a real and true phenomenon. Even though I know that death is quite simply put, a trick of the senses, I too have felt the pain as though the trick were the only reality that existed. The best conclusion I can come to surrounding this puzzle is as follows:

As long as we extend our love to only a chosen few individuals, our heart is rather like a tree with as many branches as we have loved ones. Some branches are stronger and larger than others, just as our love for some people is stronger than our love for others. But they are all branches of love, extending outward toward the object of that love. Some fortunate people have many, many branches on their tree of love and others have relatively few. The only problem with branches is that they are brittle and they break. When the object of that love is no longer present, it seems as though a very real part of us has been lost. A limb has been lopped off of our tree and the bigger the limb, the more painful the loss.

We will continue to experience the apparent loss of love as a painful event, until we can experience it not as a tree filled with branches, but rather as an ocean that flows out from our hearts and encompasses all of humanity. If our love truly embraces all souls, we will be able to ebb and flow with each one as it moves along its own path, here on earth or elsewhere. We will not experience ourselves as "separate from" others, but as one divine universal essence.

The ocean does not mourn or suffer pain when a drop of water evaporates and returns to the clouds from whence it came. The ocean knows that the drop continues to exist and that it will return, in time, after other adventures, to join the other drops that make up the sea.

I suspect that the state of loving all souls is what is referred to as spiritual enlightenment and that it was experienced by many of the great masters who have taught us with their words and deeds throughout the ages.

I imagine that my thoughts do not ease your pain, Omar and for that I am sorry because I truly would lighten your burden if I knew how. Please forgive my lack and know that I share this aspect of humanity with you.

I am confident that Spirit not only loves you and your daughter wholly and completely, but that everything allowed to transpire here in your earthly life is orchestrated for only your highest good (from a spiritual perspective). Your daughter does not want you to mourn and God does not require you to suffer. I will hold you in the light

*and remember both you and your beloved daughter in my
meditations.*

Please remember to:
Acknowledge what is,
    Accept what is,
        And respond to what is, with love.
    Yours in the light,
    W.

—

Dear Corinne,

*I'm missing both you and your father deeply today. You both
seem close in mind and much too far away from me in body and even
in Spirit. He was such a wonderful soul and he loved you so very
much. Knowing that you are in the world gives me hope. You are a
kind and loving presence on the planet and I'm so grateful to have
shared the early years of your life. I've learned more from you than
I could ever teach.*

I love you deeply and with all my heart,
    Mom

Anika sealed her latest letter to Corinne into a matching
envelope, wrote her daughter's name and the date on the outside of the envelope, and pulled a large memory book down
from the shelf. She opened the book and flipped past the
many pages filled with letters she had written to Corinne during the past several years. Then she carefully pasted this new
letter onto a blank page near the back. Anika returned the
book to its place hoping she would one day have the chance to
hand the book to her daughter herself.

The Seeker XII

"Western street coming up," the cabbie said.

Derek leaned forward and rubbed the fog off the back window with his fingertips. He peered out as the cab slowed for the turn onto Western. He was surprised to see that they weren't in the retail type neighborhood he'd expected. This looked more like a light industrial park of some kind. He double-checked the address for Starburst.

"Is this 1320 Western?" he asked as the driver slowed to a stop on the street in front of a smallish, unmarked, window-less warehouse with a large garage type loading door.

"Yep. This is it," the driver said.

"Well, I'll be dammed!" For a moment, Derek was baffled. Something wasn't right here. He had come with a plan. He was going to verify that the Denver address of Starburst was nothing but a mail drop, quit this case, and go home. That was the plan.

But this wasn't a mail drop. This was nothing like a mail drop. This place was, well, a place. That wasn't part of the plan. That wasn't part of the plan at all.

Derek needed time to think.

"Can you wait for me while I see if this is the right place?" he asked the driver.

"Sure."

The cab idled as Derek stepped out into the cold and immediately relit the cigarette still hanging from his lips. He hunched down deeply into his inadequate jacket and walked slowly around the property to get a feel for the place. 1320 was one of four small matching warehouses that shared a central parking lot. There were about three dozen employee cars in the lot and another dozen or so scattered empty parking spaces. A couple of guys leaned against the wall of the warehouse directly across the lot from 1320 and smoked.

Across the street was an identical complex. In fact, the entire, three block long, dead-end street was nothing but a series of warehouse pods like the one he was standing in front of now. The only way in or out was directly up the street two blocks to the intersection. Even then, there wasn't much there. It was another three or four blocks of empty, hilly landscape in either direction before the rest of the town seemed to kick in.

Derek walked up to the glass front door of 1320 and peered in. There was no one in the lobby. Derek tried the door. It was locked.

"They're closed," one of the smokers shouted to Derek from across the parking lot.

"Do you know when they open?" Derek shouted back. He pulled his collar up over his face both to keep warm and to stay anonymous.

The smokers looked at each other and shrugged. They shook their heads. The second one shouted, "Sometimes I seen the guy come in and out in the afternoon. Sometimes not. Don't know for sure."

"Afternoons huh?" Derek shouted back. "Thanks"

The smokers both nodded uncertainly then went back to their conversation. Derek sighed heavily and leaned thoughtfully against the locked glass door at 1320. *Shit*, he thought, *now I gotta do a stakeout in Denver?*

Derek couldn't believe his rotten luck. Anika Lucio was very likely hiding somewhere in them thar hills and with a lead like this he could hardly call and tell his client he was licked. He shivered again, cursing the cold, and pulled out his cell phone.

"Hello?" came the familiar voice on the other end of the line.

"Jack, it's me, Derek."

"Oh hey, Derek. What's up?"

"Did you find out anything new on this Paul guy?" Derek asked.

"No. Nothing really. He's a P.I. for sure, with a delivery for The Writetress, but he won't talk about his client of course," Jack said. "He's looking out here because of the Marina Del Rey postmark on some of her letters that he's heard about."

"Forget about Marina Del Rey," Derek said. "She's here in Denver. Or somewhere around here."

"For real?" Jack sounded uneasy.

"Yep. I'm standing in front of the warehouse right now. They probably just ship her outgoing stuff to the Marina and have it postmarked from there."

Jack whistled. "She's one smart lady, huh?"

"Yeah, almost too smart! But I think we're getting close. Listen, I need you to get here as soon as possible to help me with the stakeout on this place. Can you leave tonight?"

"Well, the thing is . . .uh, Derek?"

Derek didn't like the sound of Jack's voice. "What, Jack?"

"The thing is, I, uh, I'm sorry, but, uh, I don't wanna be a P.I. anymore."

"You WHAT?" Derek couldn't believe his ears.

"I don't wanna be a P.I. anymore, Derek."

"What are you talking about? Of course you wanna be a P.I.. You're only two lousy months away from getting your license, remember? Jack, you love this job. This is your next big career move. REMEMBER, Jack? Jack?" Derek was desperate.

"The thing is, I like California too much," Jack said. "I don't wanna leave."

"You don't wanna leave?" Derek screamed into the cell. "You don't wanna leave? Jack, listen to me. California is nothing but a huge, open air insane asylum, for crying out loud. Whaddya mean you don't wanna leave?"

"Aww. It's really nice out here, Derek. You should come check it out sometime."

"But what about your apartment, Jack? What about our partnership? I was gonna leave the whole entire agency to you just as soon as this gig is over, I swear. I really need you on this one, Jack."

"I know, Derek. I'm really sorry," Jack said. "Hey! You need an apartment, right? Maybe you could just, you know, take mine."

"You want me to take your apartment?"

"Sure? Why not. Take it. It's yours."

"What about all your stuff? What about the agency?"

"You can have my stuff too, Derek. I'm gonna fly back next week and pick up a few things, but you can keep the rest. I don't need it here. Sandy is setting me up in real estate. Can you believe that, Derek? I'm gonna start over and be a real estate agent in Malibu! Home of the stars. Sandy says my people skills will be perfect for real estate."

"Your *people skills?*" Derek didn't know exactly where he was standing at the moment, but it wasn't earth.

"Yeah. I'm learning to surf too." Jack sounded way too animated for Derek's nerves right now.

"Shit, Jack! What am I supposed to do now? I'm standing here in the frigging cold staring at a warehouse on a dead-end street, that I gotta case, and I got no partner to help me out."

"Aw, you can do it, Derek. You've done it a million times before I came along. I have confidence in you."

"You have *confidence in me*?" Derek couldn't take much more of this.

"Look, Jack. Just help me out this one last time. Please? I'm begging you here, Buddy. Please?"

"No can do, Derek. My real estate class meets tonight for the first time. I don't wanna miss the first day of the rest of my life, you know?" Jack chuckled. Derek nearly vomited.

"I can't believe you're doing this to me, Jack. I really *cannot* believe you're doing this."

Derek hung up the phone and resisted the strong urge to throw it across the parking lot. He tromped back to the cab with a full-blown headache now and took one last drag on his cigarette with his nearly frozen fingers before getting inside.

"Is there a cheap motel near here?" he sighed.

The Wood Man III

Anika spent much of that same Friday alternately pacing the wood floor of her small cabin, and absentmindedly straightening imaginary messes. It was quite some time before she returned to her usual state of mindfulness, and when she did, she realized she had been thinking about Danny.

Who was this peculiar young man? She had assumed he couldn't talk at all, but now realized that it was a simple matter of his rarely being compelled to do so. Could he read? Or read minds? He had certainly been aware somehow that she needed an accepting ear and a reassuring hug on his last visit.

And what did he mean "Just tell her you don't know?" How could she answer her loyal fans' earnest queries with something as unsatisfying as that? Didn't they deserve a more complete and heartfelt response? Wasn't it her job to provide it? Was this young man a simpleton or some kind of sage? What sort of thoughts did he think? What was she supposed to learn from all this mystery?

Anika's face warmed with shame when she realized that, before last week, she had never really attempted to speak with Danny, other than the initial issuing of instructions on that first day. No wonder he hadn't spoken to her. Why should he? She was only another lady who couldn't be bothered. She probably didn't notice him at all, just like all the others.

But they had exchanged smiles and shared lemonade many times, hadn't they? Anika brightened at the thought. Maybe they really were friends. She was surprised how enthusiastic she became at the thought of befriending Danny. Anika felt a familiar surge of energy within her. It was an energy that always proceeded a passionate quest, pursued with great appetite and enthusiasm. She felt it when she was pregnant with Corinne. She felt it before writing each of her first several books. She had felt it before moving up to these mountains. And she felt it now, at the sound of Danny's truck turning onto her drive.

The battered pickup made its way slowly up the incline and pulled alongside the house where the new pile of wood waited to grow. Anika stepped out onto the porch and gave a tentative half wave as the truck moved past where she was standing and continued on. She was not at all sure whether Danny had registered her greeting. She hesitated there, listening to him get out of the pickup, hearing the sound of his footsteps on the gravel drive and the bang of the tailgate as it dropped open for its master.

Why don't I just go down there? she wondered as she gazed, motionless, at the three, wooden stairs.

"Hi!"

Anika started at the booming voice. Looking up, she saw the top half of Danny, his arms holding logs, peeking around the corner of the cabin, between the wooden slats of the porch rail. He gave her a broad, gap toothed grin and disappeared back around the house before she had the sense to reply.

Anika blinked, blindsided again by the wood man. *Danny is a hit-and-run talker*, she thought, and the thought brought a smile to her face. She trotted down the stairs and fairly skipped around the corner to watch him work.

He was already sweating when she got there.

At a loss for words, she blurted out, "can I help?"

He paused in his efforts just long enough to size her up.

"Nah," he replied after a beat, as he shook his head, "City girls don't carry wood right." Then he resumed his work without so much as a hint as to how Anika should react.

Anika blinked, not sure whether to take offense or laugh. Danny had seemed to be making neither joke nor cruel remark, but just calling things as he saw them with no judgment attached. After a moment, Anika decided to smile, and thought of how she must look to Danny's eyes.

"How do you know I'm a city girl?" she asked after watching him awhile longer. "Maybe I was raised in the country and moved to the city after I grew up."

"You planted a tree 'top your septic tank," Danny said. He stopped working and straightened up before pointing to a small spruce nearby. "Only city girls would do that."

Anika felt her face heat up as she turned and gazed with dread at the four-foot conifer she had so lovingly planted alongside the house just a month after moving into the cabin. Danny must have noticed her dismay.

"I can move it for you. Just don't wait too long."

Anika dismissed Danny's time-sensitive afterthought as having to do with the size of the tree or the oncoming winter and nothing more, as she brightened at his offer of help. He was already stacking wood again by the time she was able to reply.

"That would be great," she said. "When can you come by?"

"Tuesday." He smashed the tailgate closed on his pickup. Then he hoisted a few logs and stood waiting with his arms full for Anika to make the first move toward the porch. Her mind still on next Tuesday, she didn't react.

"Lemonade?" he asked.

Anika was startled, "Oh! Yes. Sure. Come on in." She led the way to the porch with Danny following.

Their lemonade ritual proceeded silently and unchanged as before, and Danny was in his pickup with the motor running before Anika spoke again.

"See you Tuesday, then," she called as he drove past the porch on his way down the drive.

He grinned and gunned the engine.

Anika stood watching the drive long after Danny's truck had disappeared. *See you Tuesday,* she smiled to herself. She could see now that Danny was far more than he appeared to be. He was smart, for one thing, and seemed wise, for another. Definitely aware and mindful and smart and wise, and Anika shook her head in wonder at the beautiful sense of humor present everywhere in the universe.

—

Hi Honey,

I've been remembering the songs we used to sing together when you were little and I just wanted to thank you for being a part of my life. I'm glad you're on the planet and I'm imagining us together.
    Love,
    Mom

P.S. I thought of you all day on your birthday. When I see you next we'll go shopping together and you can pick out a gift.

The Homosexual

Dear Writetress,

My son is a faggot! I raised the kid right and he turns out a stinking faggot. I don't know whether to kill him or kill myself. It makes me want to puke all the goddamn time. I just can't believe it's true. I gave him everything in life, and look what he does with it! I loved that kid so much and now I can never let him come home again. Why would he hate me so much that turns into a disgusting freak? What does your fancy spiritual mumbo jumbo say about faggots? I know what the Bible says in the story of Sodom and Gomorrah. It's not right with God to be queer.

William Sandoval

—

Dear William,

I can feel the pain and rage and disgust in your words and I commend you for your courage to express them on paper. Your son has shocked you with this news and you have no idea what to do about it. You loved him and raised him the best you could, and yet he has disappointed you. The fact that you've written to me tells me a lot. It tells me that, even though you are very angry and disappointed right now, you really do love your son, and want help coming to terms with what has happened in your life. You are expressing your anger, and that is a great first step. But know this: it is only the first step. There is more work that you must do inside yourself, if you want to move past this place of pain in your life.

You are revolted by the idea of homosexuality so much that you've cast out your own son rather than revisit that issue within yourself. On the one hand, you love him completely; on the other, he represents something completely unacceptable to you. It is the tension between those two opposites that is causing you so much anguish.

Before you choose to align yourself with an idea, rather than a real human being, I urge you to consider that this is still your son, your beloved boy, and that he needs you now more than ever. This must be a difficult time for him too — maybe the most difficult in his life. The loving support of a father can mean a lot to a child, and driving him away will only hurt you both. This is not something he has chosen to do in order to hurt you. It is ok to be angry, it is ok to be hurt, it is ok to express those things, but please keep the lines of communication open between you. Do it for your own sake if you can't do it for him. The things you are feeling will eat you alive if you don't let them out. I'm sure he expected a strong reaction when he told you, but he still had the courage to let you know. Please have the courage to keep your son in your life. God has put him there for a reason and it is my conviction is that it was <u>not</u> for you to reject him.

Please do not use your belief in the Christian faith as an excuse for denying your son. The Bible tells us many different things about how God would like us to live, and we know that not one of us is perfect when it comes to following all of the guiding principles it contains. We do know that the overall message of Christ's teaching is one of love and acceptance for each other; not judgment, not criticism, and not anger. If I understand it correctly, the Bible teaches us to love each other, regardless of our perceived "failings" and to leave the rest to God. We are here to do the best we can — not to judge others as they struggle to do the same.

Regardless of how you feel about homosexuality, it can't be your place to judge your son here on this earth. This boy is a human being and God made him the way that he is. God has also told us to love each other. If there are judgments to be made, let's leave them up to our Creator. For the sake of your health, your own Spiritual growth, and your relationship with your son, I urge you to consider moving through your anger to the brighter spots that lie on the other side.

I will hold you and your son in the light during my meditations and I wish you all the best.

Please remember to:

Acknowledge what is,

Accept what is,

And respond to what is, with love.

Yours in the light,

W.

The Obvious Question

Dear writetress,

 If God is so loving and we are all composed of a divine inner Soul as your books say, why is there so much suffering in the world? Why are people so cruel to each other? Why are there wars? Why are there homeless and poor people and sick children? It seems like God lets a lot of people down.

 Sincerely,
 Rosa Sanchez

—

Dear Rosa,

 Thank you for writing. You ask a lot of good questions. I believe God loves us enough to give us freedom of choice. It is our choice to come to this planet and it is our prerogative to experience the type of life that will provide us with the most opportunities to learn whatever it is we've come here for. We each develop our own curriculum for this earth school and it is neither useful nor even possible for us to judge another's path.

 If we but truly remember that we are composed of a divine inner core, the rest of human experience becomes but a stage play, acted out in this theater called earth. The difficulty comes when we forget our true divine essence. When that happens, the earth events that we participate in can seem frighteningly real, but they ultimately have no more or less significance than any class taken at any other school along the way.

There is suffering in the world because we have forgotten that we are Souls. We have forgotten that our physical world reality is not our true higher reality and we behave as though it were. There are poor and sick and homeless people in the world to remind us that compassion and service are our true nature. There is cruelty in the world because people are in pain from forgetting their own worth and beauty. The only way to end suffering and poverty and cruelty is with love. Unconditional, universal love and forgiveness for ourselves and for each other. Fortunately, since love is at the core of our basic makeup, it is always there for us to access within ourselves.

Our true inner nature remains pure and unaffected by our experiences here on earth. We learn or we don't learn, but it doesn't really matter. We are always loved and we can never really die. So please begin today to focus on adding your contribution to the sum total of light and love in the world. Be careful not to add to the sum total of anger and violence and hatred. Even subtle judgments practiced against yourself contribute darkness where light is desperately needed.

Wherever you see suffering, you are being called to apply love. Do whatever feels right for you; send money, lend a helping hand, offer a smile or a kind word. Know that your one light, shining brightly, can and does make a difference. The more of us there are who are willing to stand for peace and compassion and forgiveness, to spread our love and light without apology, the less there will be suffering in the world. Please join us in the light.

I send you all my love and heartfelt thanks for writing to me.

Please remember to:
Acknowledge what is,
Accept what is,
And respond to what is, with love.
Yours in the light,
W.

The Wood Man IV

Anika arose from her rocker just as Danny's truck came up the drive. She instantly felt better at the sound of the engine and the crunch of the tires on the ground as he pulled up in front of the house. This time there was no wood in the back of the pickup. Danny parked and got out of the truck, pulling on his work gloves as he always did. He retrieved a small box from the passenger side of the pickup and held it up for Anika to see.

My mom made you a pie," he shouted a little louder than necessary. "Apple. Probably good."

Anika smiled and headed down to accept the gift.

"Will you tell your mother thank you for me?" she asked.

Danny grinned and grabbed a shovel from the bed of the pickup.

"Where you want it?" he asked.

It took Anika a beat to figure out what Danny meant.

"Oh, the tree. I was thinking it would look nice over there." She pointed to a spot in the clearing in front of the house. "What do you think?"

"It's a tree." Danny said as he started toward the spot. "Gonna look the same no matter where you put it."

Anika smiled as Danny started to dig. She knew that transplanting a four-foot tall tree was going to take a bit longer than unloading a truck full of wood, so she headed inside to prepare a mid-task round of refreshments for Danny.

When she returned to the hole-in-progress with a tray of warm cider and croissants, Danny was sweating in the cold air. His breath steamed out like small white clouds in short panting bursts. He gladly stopped for a drink.

"How's it going," asked Anika.

"It's a hole," Danny shrugged.

Danny finished his cider and began digging again. Anika didn't know what else to do, so she went back to the porch and pretended to answer more mail while she watched Danny work.

He approached this task with the same mindfulness that he brought to stacking wood. He dug slowly and methodically and appeared to be wholly absorbed in what he was doing. Every now and then, he would bend down and inspect the hole he was digging. Occasionally she saw him gently remove an earthworm or other tiny creature from harm's way before continuing to dig. Anika marveled at his patience and kindness. *Zen and the Art of Manual Labor*, she thought and smiled to herself. She felt fortunate once again to be watching a Master at work.

It was dusk when he finished and came to the house to wash his hands. He was breathing hard through his mouth, with a veil of sweat on his forehead.

"Would you like to stay for awhile? asked Anika. "I could make us some dinner."

Danny just shook his head. It seemed too much effort for him to speak. He washed his hands, drank a glass of water and left rather quickly through the front door.

"The tree looks great over there. Thank you," Anika called after him.

Without turning back, Danny raised his hand in a backward wave, got into his truck and drove away. Anika didn't know what to think. He hadn't seemed angry, but something was definitely wrong. She was disappointed that he hadn't stayed, since she had been looking forward to having a chat of some kind with him.

Oh well, she thought, *there's always tomorrow.*

The Seeker XIII

Derek sat freezing in the warehouse parking lot. The heater in the crappy station wagon from the local Rent-a-Wreck didn't work as well as the rental agent had imagined it would. Derek wasn't surprised, just cold and miserable and feeling very foul.

He had been at it for seven days now, not counting the weekends, and was afraid he might be running out of time. He still had a several weeks to go to meet his client's mid-December deadline, but he had slipped-up when he told Jack where Anika Lucio was. Jack might tell Sandy. Derek suspected it wouldn't be long after that before Sandy told the mysterious Paul. And Derek didn't want company in the parking lot of 1320. Not that kind of company, anyway.

It was a tricky stakeout to be sure. In the parking lot, he had to rely on the workers who came and went at all hours, to assume he was an employee of one of the other warehouses on the property. He parked in roughly the same empty spot each day so as not to garner undue attention by trespassing in someone else's favorite place. Then he sat in the car all day, watching 1320, and waiting.

He had seen a lot. He knew, for instance, that the post office delivered the mail bags, forwarded from New York no doubt, to 1320 between noon and one o'clock each weekday. He knew that there was a little old man inside who would unlock the front door for the mail carrier, and then lock it up again. Derek had never seen the old man arrive, and guessed he showed up sometime shortly before Derek himself in the morning. Within twenty minutes of bringing in the mail, the old guy would leave 1320 via the front door, carrying nothing but a thermos, get into his car in the parking lot and drive away.

A pattern was emerging. Twice during the seven days, last Tuesday and again on Friday, a black 4Runner with black windows had pulled up to the building at approximately three pm, opened the large shipping door via remote, and pulled inside before closing the door behind itself. Derek had never seen the driver. Both times, the door had opened again about fifteen minutes later, allowing the 4Runner to pull out of the building and leave the parking lot, before automatically closing itself again in the wake of the mysterious vehicle.

Derek knew Anika Lucio's mail was in that black SUV. He also knew he'd have to follow it if he wanted to find her. The trick was doing it without blowing his cover.

The row of warehouses was always pretty quiet when the SUV left. The afternoon shifts started at three thirty and the day shift didn't leave until four. The few early arrivals who were clocking in for afternoons were coming in, not going out of the dead-end warehouse row at that time. A beat-up old station wagon tailing a black SUV very far under these circumstances would be pretty dammed obvious.

Today was Tuesday again. If the 4Runner showed like last week, Derek knew what he had to do. But for now, he waited.

It wasn't getting any warmer in Denver, and he had purchased a new, down jacket in green camouflage color, that was surprisingly comfortable. It would never fly in New York of course, but the military motif was a big one in Denver and the jacket had been on sale. People here didn't seem to care what they looked like as long as they were warm. After being in town for a week and a half now in October, Derek whole-heartedly concurred.

Around two thirty, just as Derek was opening his second pack of cigarettes for the day, his phone rang. It was Jack.

"Hey, Derek. It's me. Jack."

Derek lit up. "Hey, Jack." He hadn't quite forgiven Jack for bailing on him, but he was starting to understand the appeal of a warm climate about now.

"I'm in New York, just clearing a few things out of my apartment. I see you ain't been staying here."

"Yeah," Derek replied.

"You still in Denver?"

"Yep."

"Wow! How's it going?" Jack asked.

"What do you care?" Derek exploded, "Like you could give a rat's ass how I'm doing."

"Sorry. Sorry." Jack paused for a beat before continuing. "Hey, do you want the apartment or not? I gotta get everything cleared outta here today if you ain't paying October rent, which is already late."

"Go ahead and clear it out," Derek sighed. "I think I'm gonna be here awhile and I haven't made any money yet. I never liked your apartment anyhow."

"Yeah, like yours was such a penthouse," Jack said.

Derek smiled in spite of himself and thought that maybe he felt a little better. It was good to hear Jack's voice again, even if he was a no good California beach bum now.

"Whaddya want me to do with your stuff?" Jack asked.

"Oh. Yeah," Derek remembered the three cab trips worth of junk at Jack's. "I dunno. Whaddya gonna do with yours?" he asked.

"Just put it in storage, I guess," Jack said. "It's not that much stuff. I'll get rid of the furniture."

"Yeah, you know what?" Derek sighed. "I don't really care what you do with it. Just put it in storage with your stuff, okay?"

"Sure, Derek. Sure. Anything you want."

"Hey, throw the office junk in there too, will you?" Derek asked. "It's not much, just the computer and a few papers. Looks like I won't be making rent on that place either." He sighed heavily.

"Yeah, sure, no problem," Jack assured him. "Uh, Derek?"

"Yeah?"

"You mind if I keep the rest of those Writetress books in there? You know, take 'em back with me to Malibu? Sandy's crazy about The Writetress and I want to be sure I've read all her stuff. I kinda like it too. It's pretty good."

"Sure. Help yourself. I don't ever want to see 'em again anyway," Derek said. There was an awkward pause and then Derek remembered, "Hey, how's that real estate class going?"

He was only trying to be polite, and as soon as he asked the question, Derek was sorry. Jack launched into a way too animated description of contract clauses and pricing strategies that just wasn't worth the cell time. At the first possible break in Jack's monologue Derek excused himself, saying he had to get back to work, and hung up. When it came to sitting in a cold car in a warehouse parking lot in Denver, or listening to someone talk about real estate while sitting in a cold car in a warehouse parking lot in Denver, he'd take sitting in a cold car in a warehouse parking lot in Denver any day.

The call had been a reasonable diversion though, and at three o'clock, just as Derek hoped, the black 4Runner drove up and disappeared into the warehouse. As soon as the loading door shut behind the vehicle, Derek got out of his car and nonchalantly leaned against the other building's wall, near the side entrance, where he lit up a cigarette and kept his eyes on 1320.

When the loading door began to open, Derek took his last drag and stubbed out the butt with his toe. Then he headed casually toward his car at a relaxed pace as if he had just left the other building.

Today he would follow the 4Runner as far as he could easily go without being detected. On Friday, he'd be parked along the route in a different Rent-a-Wreck special, and pick up the chase again when the SUV passed the point where he'd left off three days before. Each Tuesday and Friday he would follow another easy portion of the route in a different rental car, always being careful not to be obvious, until the SUV led him right to Anika Lucio's door. It wasn't the greatest plan in the world, but at least it wouldn't blow his cover. It might take a couple weeks, it might take a month, but if Anika Lucio was anywhere nearby, it just might work. Besides, Derek couldn't think of anything better, and at least he could take the next couple days off.

Restlessness

The next morning, Anika was up early. She smiled when she looked out the front window of her cabin and saw the freshly planted tree that Danny had moved for her yesterday. It looked wonderful and she decided to be happy. After all, he would be back today with another load of wood. It was going to be a good day.

She caught herself wondering what Danny might be doing right that very moment. *Why am I so interested in this particular young man?* she wondered to herself as she hummed and made up a fresh batch of lemonade.

Maybe you'd be just as excited to see any human being, came the internal reply.

Truth be told, Anika had gotten more than she bargained for when she first moved up to the mountains three-quarters of a year ago. She knew the transition wouldn't be easy, which was why she had made it so utterly complete. By selling her homes and furnishings, The Writetress had made sure it would be no simple feat to return to civilization the first time she got restless in her self-imposed exile.

And restless she had gotten. Although she was growing more used to it now, it still wasn't quite the tranquil life she had fantasized about. Mountain life was hard and the air was dry. In the winter, there would be weeks of being snowed in. Many of the products and services she had become accustomed to were not easily available here. And although the peace and serenity she had craved were all around her in the neighboring wilderness, her insides had yet to settle in and find harmony with her surroundings.

The Writetress was a city girl, born and bred, who had always craved the simple life she imagined rural living would bring. Growing up in Chicago, she had dreamed of riding horses in the woods, though she had never actually ridden. When her adult life as a famous author grew more and more public it had grown more and more complicated as well. When people started attributing powers to her that she knew only too well that she didn't have, it had seemed like a daring escape was in order. Now she was well into her personal mission of touching her fans one-by-one instead of en masse, but she was still having doubts about her choice – and still denying them vigorously.

What else could I have done? She wondered. *They thought I was some kind of miracle worker. I had to leave, or sooner or later they'd find me out, brand me a fraud and grow angry at me. An angry mob is not my idea of a good time.*

Anika felt a subtle shame over the fact that she hadn't easily settled into the inner peace she had anticipated would be so easy to find in this beautiful place. She had never openly faced her own restlessness, but it seemed to linger nonetheless. And so, it had gone for nearly nine months now. Inner peace, she had assumed, would just take more time, but as time passed, she grew more and more anxious . . . and now there was Danny.

He was her friend. He was someone she could look forward to seeing. He didn't care what the papers said about her. He didn't expect her to be superhuman. He was just another human being who liked her for what she really was.

Or was it something more than that? He was different, to be sure, but Anika suspected there was something special about Danny himself that she just hadn't figured out yet. She was certain he had been sent from Spirit with a special lesson just for her.

Fueled by her restless energy, Anika made sure the simple cabin got an extra thorough cleaning in the morning. It was nearly noon before she made it out to the porch to take on today's round of letters. Anika went through her usual centering ritual and selected a letter from her mailbag:

Dear Writetress,

Where are you? I've been waiting for your next book for months and now I hear that you have nothing new scheduled to come out yet. The whole world is wondering where you are. Are you taking a long vacation or what? Please write something new soon!

Sincerely,
Abel James

Anika felt herself bristle at the letter and more than a bit annoyed at Abel James. She concluded that she had not properly settled herself into her meditation before selecting it. Danny's impending visit was obviously on her mind and keeping her from centering herself properly. She had been thinking about once again inviting him to dinner instead of reading mail this day.

After a brief consideration, The Writetress did something she had never done before. She tossed Abel James' letter into the trash without answering it and decided this would not be a good day to read any more letters.

The Wood Man's Father

Anika made up her mind that she and Danny were going to talk today – no matter what. She was surprised at the amount of energy and thought she was putting into this young man – and she was determined to figure out why. Something was clearly special about him – but what?

When the old pickup truck turned into her drive, Anika was waiting on the porch. As the truck drew nearer, she waved. But something was wrong. The truck pulled to a stop in a different place than usual and the driver got out – but it wasn't Danny.

The old man waved to Anika and grabbed a hasty, and Anika thought, rather sloppy armload of wood.

"Where you want it?" he shouted up to her.

"What? Oh – around side the house there," Anika pointed and then hurried after this wood-bearing imposter. She arrived at the wood pile just in time to see the fellow drop his armload of wood haphazardly violating Danny's nice neat pile, and head back for another round.

"Where's Danny?" she asked.

The man stopped, then turned and put out his hand to shake. Anika took it reluctantly as he spoke.

"Hospital," he said. "I'm his pop."

"You're Danny's father? He's in the hospital? What happened? Is he all right? Anika asked anxiously, all in one concerned breath.

The old man studied her for a moment, and Anika had a brief flash of where Danny had gotten his demeanor.

"Bum ticker. Seems bad this time."

"His heart? Danny has heart problems? He never said anything." Anika suddenly remembered Danny digging holes in her yard only the day before.

"All his kind got 'em," Danny's father shrugged. "Don't live long with being that way."

Anika was shocked at both the news she was hearing and the nonchalance with which she perceived she was hearing it.

"Can he have visitors? Can I go and see him?" Anika could do nothing to quell the anxiety and sense of dread that was rising up inside of her.

Again a pause. And a stare.

"If'n you like, I suppose. Ain't no harm in it. Might like it, Danny."

"I'll go right now!" Anika turned and began to head quickly toward the house to get her keys.

"You a friend to Danny?" the old man called after her.

Anika stopped in her tracks. What was she thinking, dismissing Danny's father like that? She had been so concerned for her own obsession that she had had been disrespectful to the man standing right in her own yard. She took a deep breath and turned back.

"I'm so sorry. I didn't mean to be rude. I was just so upset to hear that Danny is ill." She extended her hand to Danny's father again.

"Let's start over. I'm Anika Lucio and yes, I am a friend of your son's."

Danny's father smiled and took her hand. "I'm Dan," he offered. "Pleased to meet you."

The two stood for an awkward beat until Dan pulled on his work gloves again and started toward the truck.

"Got wood to fetch here. You go see the boy."

"Thank you." Anika alighted like a relieved schoolgirl dismissed at the bell.

Once inside, she hastily grabbed her purse and keys and headed back out to her truck. As she headed down her driveway, she waved at Dan. He nodded; his arms full of wood on his way to mess up her perfect pile by the house.

The Healer

A nika drove almost recklessly on her way into town. She was worried about Danny and about her possible contribution to his condition. She needed to see him and to know that he was going to be all right.

She had never been inside the town's small medical facility, though she knew where it was. There was an information desk inside the front door.

"May I help you?" the volunteer retiree asked.

"I'm here to see a patient. His name is Danny . . ." Anika stopped cold, realizing in horror that she didn't even know Danny's last name. How was she going to find her friend?

"Sure," the helper smiled. "Everybody in town knows Danny. He's down the hall in room thirty-two," the woman pointed the way.

"Thank you," Anika called over her shoulder as she hurried into the world of linoleum and antiseptic smells that reminded her strongly of when her own mother had been terminally ill. She shook her memories off at the door to room thirty-two, where she paused and took a deep breath before pushing it open.

"Please let him be okay," she prayed absentmindedly as her eyes fell upon the foot of the bed nearest the door.

The room was quiet, punctuated only by the sounds that hospital machines make. The far bed of the semi-private room was empty. As Anika's vision adjusted, she saw him sleeping there. Danny's eyes were closed, and as usual, his mouth half open. Although his breathing seemed a bit labored, he appeared to be comfortable, with only a minimum of tubes running in and out of his body at various angles. It was difficult to assess his coloring in the half-light seeping in from around the edges of the heavy gray curtain that covered the window on the other side of the room. Anika took a seat on the torn vinyl chair beside the bed and closed her eyes in silent prayer.

When she opened her eyes again, Danny was wide awake and looking at her. He gave a weak, half smile.

"Hi," she said.

"Hi yourself."

"Danny – don't go, okay? I mean, I need you!" Anika was startled by her own sudden outburst.

"Pop'll bring the wood" Danny managed with some effort.

"It's not the wood, Danny – it's you. I need you. I really look forward to seeing you every time you come."

No response from Danny. Anika wasn't sure whether he was too week or too stunned. She rushed to fill in the silence.

"Ever since I came out here from the city I've been holed up in my cabin all alone. You're the first person to come and see me up there. I really like it when you come."

Still no response. Anika thought she saw a faint smile but she wasn't sure. The peace in the room wasn't inside her heart, so she didn't notice it and continued, in full confession mode now.

"I figured I could escape the problems of my life by simplifying, you know? No more books, no more media interviews, no more publishers and editors and lawyers, no more reporters with their tall tales, no more ridiculous expectations from the public, no more nothing. Just me and my thoughts and my correspondence. I thought I was fine up here alone in the mountains. No more problems."

"Guess you brought the problem with you."

Danny labored to voice the words, but he spoke with such certainty and force that they struck Anika like a physical blow.

She knew he was on to something as she collapsed in her chair and fought back the tears that suddenly stung her eyes, but there was no time to respond. Danny had given her his final gift.

Anika watched as if from a great dimensional distance as the machines around her began to scream and the hospital staff rushed in. They pushed her out of the way and converged on the lifeless body. They shouted his name and pounded his chest and stuck needles in his arm. It seemed instantaneous and oddly slow all at the same time. Anika floated out of the room and found herself back at home before she was aware of being anywhere at all.

"**D**o you have any rooms available?" Derek asked.

"Yes, we do," replied the clerk at the only motel in town.

It was a snowy Friday in mid-November, when he checked into a room in the tiny mountain town, whose eight hundred residents lived high above and far from Denver for some strange reason that Derek could neither fathom nor appreciate.

His plan was working, he could feel it. It had taken him nearly a month, but he had traced the SUV's route, day-by-day in one rental car after another, to the base of the main road that ran up this mountain out of the city.

There were three small towns on the road, before the ridge, and countless private properties tucked in between them. This place was in the middle. But Derek already knew he was getting close. Last Friday, he had watched the SUV drive up right through the bottom town and keep on going. On Tuesday he had waited in the uppermost town, but the SUV hadn't made it that far. Derek was confident that Anika Lucio was somewhere in between, very close to where he was now. Today he would stand casually out by the main road and see whether the SUV went right through the town or not. Then he would know whether to look lower or higher on the hill for his missing person. In the meantime, he could start asking questions.

He lit up a cigarette and decided to take a walk around the tiny shopping district. He had exhausted all the Denver Rent-A-Wreck inventory in the past few weeks, and was back to driving the original crappy station wagon. It wasn't exactly a comfortable car, so it felt good to stand up, and move around while exploring the town a bit.

Not that there was much of anything there. Derek never had understood how people of any level of sophistication could stand to live in a town without Starbucks coffee or Wolfgang Puck pizza. At the very least, he'd require a multi-plex movie theater and a decent bookstore wherever he was going to stay for long. As if on cue, just as Derek had the thought, he turned a corner and there was a little hole-in-the-wall used bookstore. Something about it, maybe just the cold weather outside, pulled him in.

A bell tinkled on the door as Derek entered and shook off the snow. There were two or three other shoppers casually browsing the stacks of books and keeping warm. A woman behind the cash registered called out to Derek.

"Hi there. Can I help you?"

"Yeah, I'm uh, looking for a book by Anika . . .uh, The Writetress. Do you have anything by her?"

The woman looked pleased, "We certainly do." She came out from behind the counter and led Derek to a back corner of the room. "Here you go." She gestured to a shelf-and-a-half of the very same books Derek had left behind in his office in New York.

"Great. Thanks," said Derek. "I hear she lives around here," he added casually, watching closely for a reaction.

Derek got what he was looking for. At first the woman appeared excited and about to say one thing, and then quickly changed her mind. She regarded Derek suspiciously. "I wouldn't know anything about that," she said flatly and walked away, leaving Derek behind to browse the stacks. He quickly grabbed the nearest Writetress book without even looking at the title, paid for it with cash, and left the store so as not to blow his cover.

It was the same everywhere he went with one small difference. When he asked about The Writetress, no one seemed to react at all except for the woman in the book store. In fact, half the people he asked had never heard of such a person. Derek guessed that people there didn't really get out all that much. But when he changed his tactics and started asking about Anika Lucio, and did she live near here, he got much the same reaction from the other townspeople as he had from the bookseller. About all he was able to discern was that there was definitely someone named Anika living somewhere around here, and no one in town trusted him enough to say who it was or where she might be. It looked like he might have to extend his stay in lovely middle-of-nowhere, Colorado for a while. Derek shivered at the thought.

It was nearly dusk when the black SUV rolled up the main road and kept on going right past where Derek was standing. He watched it climb the hill for a while before turning away. He now knew that Anika Lucio was hiding up there somewhere, and apparently, not very far up there. He had narrowed it down to a five-mile uphill stretch of rural road. He would drive up the hill tomorrow and see if anything obvious caught his eye. Worst he could do was find a place to park and wait for the SUV again on Tuesday afternoon, and who knows, he might even do better than that.

The Jerk

Dear Writetress,

My boss is a big fat jerk. He is rude, insulting and just plain mean. He is ok to everyone else, but he treats me awful. He singles me out for abuse. It's not fair and he's an idiot. I have been looking for another job for months but have not found one yet. I'm thinking of getting a lawyer to sue him for mental distress or something. My girlfriend reads your books and says I should ask you what to do. I told her you don't know my boss but she made me write anyway, so here's my letter. Do you think I should sue the loser?

Sincerely,
Adam Winston, Jr.

Anika smiled as she chose a brilliant gold parchment for her first letter since Danny died several weeks ago. She was sitting indoors in front of a blazing fire, having spent all that time in mourning and solitude. She hadn't been too sure about getting back to the mail that had been piling up, but Spirit had clearly granted her an easy one to get started with again. No meditation required for this reply. She shook her head and began to write.

Dear Adam,

What a wonderful favor your boss is doing for you!

This may not win me any popularity contests, but I think your boss is doing you a great service by treating you in a way that you perceive as being unfair. What a grand opportunity to look inside yourself and see just why it is that you regard his treatment as inappropriate when your colleagues obviously don't. Allow me to suggest that perhaps your boss is acting as a mirror to you, of some inner quality or qualities that you actually dislike about yourself.

Whenever we have any hidden, unresolved issues within our subconscious (or even conscious) mind, they will surely show up as irritation toward someone else. The best way I know to find those troublesome issues within, is to look without at the things that disturb our peace.

The ink was not yet dry on page one as Anika set her pen to a second sheet of stationery. She was on a roll.

Whenever your peace has been disturbed, in that moment you are faced with a very holy choice. A great teacher of Spiritual lessons once said, "How you relate to the issue, is the issue." This event in your life isn't about your boss's behavior; it is about how you choose to react to that behavior. If you choose to respond by searching within to the place inside you that resonates with the image that you hold of your boss, you have an opportunity to heal that issue for the last time. If you choose to practice the alternate course of blaming your boss for your unhappiness, and perhaps pursuing a legal battle, I wish you much joy and happiness in that choice of action as well. There is no right or wrong approach. I do want to assure you, however, that if you choose not to heal the issue within, it will continue to appear without, most likely as yet another person who

*provides you with the same irritating service as your boss does now
— only more so.*

*What a joyous opportunity you have! Please be sure to examine
the issue with great compassion and gratitude, both toward your boss
and yourself. Remember to apply loving and kindhearted forgiveness
to yourself for your own perceived shortcomings, and your boss, for
his.*

*I wish you only what you most wish for yourself, at your deepest
and most spiritual inner level.*

*Please remember to:
Acknowledge what is,
Accept what is,
And respond to what is, with love.
Yours in the light,
W.*

Anika felt a small pride in the speed and certainty of her
response. She finished her letter to Adam, sealed it into a
beautiful matching orange envelope without even re-reading
it, then burst into laughter when she realized that Adam
would never see her brilliant reply.

He had not included a return address.

For a moment Anika was amused, and then it dawned on
her, as it eventually always did, that this choice of letter was no
accident. She felt a faint sense of dread as she realized that the
lesson here, whatever it was, must be one for her and her
alone.

Oh damn! Anika cringed as she gingerly opened the letter
and reread her own words. She felt again the wave of spiritual
superiority that she had felt while setting ink to paper. Only
this time, the feeling was mirrored back to her as a lesson and
she had to shake her head in wonder at the perfection of the

universe for not allowing Adam to read her arrogantly written reply. It was obvious from her choice of words that she had felt herself more spiritually advanced than her would be reader. She had judged his path to be less enlightened than her own. She was disgusted with herself and sighed in shame as she realized her smugness.

Although she still believed in the truth of the words she had written, Anika knew that if she was going to be an advocate for love and compassion, she had better practice them herself. It was hardly going to be useful to Adam or anyone else to be preached to from on high. If she were going to judge her readers, she would never be able to help them heal themselves or anyone else. In fact, if she was going to judge her readers, she had no business writing to them in the first place.

Maybe I really am a fraud. If only Danny was here, she thought for at least the thousandth time. *If only Danny was here.*

After Danny's passing, Anika had spent her time erecting some very flattering memories of the boy. She had bemoaned the loss of his perceived wisdom and had generously infused her memory of him with a number of extraordinary qualities that she couldn't help but miss. Danny had been more than a simple-minded and conscientious stacker of wood. He had been a mindful, aware, and enlightened being sent to wake her from her own pathetic self-deceptions. If only she had paid more attention to him while he was here. If only she had spent more time talking with him, to garner more of his precious wisdom. Of course, she had thrown in liberal amounts of self-blame over allowing Danny to transplant her tree for her – which of course – must have been what killed him. All in all, Anika had wallowed in near-perfect misery for the last several months, and was no longer confident of anything about herself, least of all her letters.

Feeling unworthy of her self-appointed mission and steeped in self-doubt, Anika decided to take the rest of the afternoon off and go for a walk in the cold, mountain air. She needed to take some time to work her own process of inner healing and self-forgiveness. If she succeeded, she might write again tomorrow. If not, perhaps it would be time to move on to some other way of life. There was always wood to be stacked after all.

The Walk

Anika sighed and snuggled down into her warm jacket as she stepped heavily off the porch onto the snow and frozen earth. She needed to get back to feeling good about herself, but it wasn't going to be easy. This was the same issue she had faced before. Out there. In the world. She had left the limelight for just this reason: she was tired of feeling like a fraud, tired of doing everyone's spiritual work for them and feeling somehow superior and inferior all at the same time.

The sound of her footsteps crunching on the snow startled a young deer in the yard and the deer in turn startled Anika who had been so absorbed in judging herself that she hadn't even noticed it foraging there. It didn't take long for her to lose her awareness once more and resume mulling over her situation.

As she walked, Anika recalled the early days when she was a neophyte novelist unprepared for the changes fame would visit upon her life. Oh, she enjoyed them, no doubt about that. Who wouldn't like the first-class travel and occasional limousine ride? The television and radio appearances, coupled with massive book sales and large checks only served to convince Anika that she had something worthwhile to say. And say it she had.

Looking back, Anika realized that she had acquired quite a taste for telling people how to advance their lives spiritually.

Much like a celebrity minister, her fans had flocked to her with their issues and Anika had generously supplied the answers, in the form of her many volumes of Spiritual sustenance. When her fans had endowed her with so many wonderful powers beyond even those of her own imagination, she had judged herself to be inadequate. Inadequate because she couldn't walk on water. Inadequate because she couldn't heal the sick. Even her own books began to sound hollow to her. She concluded that she wasn't doing anyone any favors by spewing out more bookshelf filler on the subject. She had plenty of money, she reasoned, so from now on she would just touch people one-on-one, in a more personal way. Thus was her escape rationalized.

Oh, she had done it all in grand and perfect Writetress style. Sold all holdings, severed all ties. Even now, no one really knew where she was. It had all been perfect, except for one small detail. She still felt like a restless imposter in the work of Spiritual teaching.

As a wise man once told her: She had brought the problem to the mountain with her.

The Writetress in Anika knew that Adam Winston, Jr. had performed a great service for her that day, but somehow, she couldn't find it in herself to be appreciative just yet. She needed to beat herself up a bit first. She knew that she would need to forgive herself later, but right now, she wanted to wallow in shame and in judgment of herself, of her books, of her arrogance and of her foolish attempt to escape to the wilds, thinking that it would solve something, all the while knowing better.

After a time, Anika squatted down to rest against the trunk of a massive spruce. She had walked without awareness for at least half a mile. The aspen grove had thinned where the conifers had thickened and Anika realized that she didn't really know this part of the woods. She suspected that she had wandered off of her own property, and decided to take a break to get her bearings. Picking absentmindedly at a frozen pinecone she found half buried in the snow, her mind turned again to the problem she had brought to the mountain.

Anika knew the issue was an old one. She had struggled with her own perceived lack of self-worth for a long time. No one understood how the famous novelist who was living the life of ease and adored by so many could ever doubt herself for a minute, but doubt she did. Self-doubt had driven her to the woods and now it was in danger of driving her right back out again.

She closed her eyes and listened for a long time to the wind song playing about her. She drew up her jacket and huddled within it as she prayed for assistance and pondered the issue she couldn't seem to escape on her own.

Maybe I could sell shoes, thought Anika to herself. *At least that's a profession that provides a genuine service to people.* But even as she had the thought, she knew that her calling was one of words, and she would have to honor it somehow. But how?

Again, she knew the answer even as she asked the question. It didn't matter what she wrote, she was not going to find the reassurances she longed for from without. Accolades and compliments from the press and her fans could hide the issue briefly and make her feel better for a time, but as long as she was carrying internal doubts about her own self-worth, she would never be able to express her thoughts freely and authentically with the true voice of love and compassion for the world.

"What made me think I had anything of value to say to people in the first place?" Anika wondered aloud, amazed at the arrogance of it all.

"What makes anyone think they have anything of value to say to anyone?" her mind echoed in a Voice that sounded surprisingly like Danny's – only now, far more articulate. Anika looked up sharply. There was no one there. Was the Voice coming from outside of her head or inside? Somewhere in the very air around her? She decided to test the sound again and continued with her half of the conversation.

"I can't tell people how to live their lives," she said aloud. She started at hearing her own words, which were quickly absorbed by the woods around her.

"Why can't you?" came the reply.

"Because I'm not even sure how I want to live my own!" she said without thinking.

"And . . ." prompted the Voice

"And because I don't want to! It all boils down to saying the same simple things over and over again, and yet people think it has to be so complicated," Anika said.

"Yet you know you must write," said the wind.

"You know you must write," echoed the trees and the forest around her.

"But why?" she cried. "Why must I write? They hang on my every word as though it were written by someone more than human. As though I were some kind of divine presence living here among them." Anika shivered in the cold.

"And aren't you?" came the soft, unmistakable reply.

The epiphany hit Anika hard.

"Of course," she whispered to herself, "of course. It's what I've been telling everyone else all along, isn't it?"

"And you've never owned it fully for yourself," answered the air.

"And I never owned it fully for myself," echoed Anika, stunned by the power of the insight.

"You are a divine being having a human experience, and a rather extraordinary one at that." The Voice, echoing words she had so often written for others, was compassionate and loving, and its recitation moved Anika to tears.

"All these years I've been telling others about their own divinity and denying my own," she sobbed. "I even got impatient with them at times when they failed to see how very special they were – each and every one of them," she felt a subtle shame as the admission crossed her lips.

"Be kind to yourself," urged the Voice. "Forgive. Release the judgments. Move forward in your loving. You have all the tools you need. You've been offering them up to your readers for years."

"I guess we really do teach best what we most need to learn," Anika sighed.

"And you've taught it well," came the response, "you've made enormous contributions to many people's lives."

"And all it's really ever been about is figuring out my own."

Anika shook her head in wonder at the elegance of a universe that had put a lesson so plainly under her nose. It couldn't have been more clear if it had been written down in black and white and placed directly in front of her face. In fact, it had. She had been the one writing it, over and over, for years. The impact of the realization was staggering.

Anika sat in silent forgiveness of herself for a long time before the wind began to pick up and the air grew colder. She thrust her hands into her jacket pockets for warmth and felt something there. She pulled out a folded piece of paper that she had stuffed in there so many months and a lifetime ago.

```
Dear Writetress,
   How do you know that the things you are saying
   are true?
Sincerely,
Helen Parker
```

A slow smile woke up Anika's face as she spoke aloud.

"Helen, I have absolutely no idea!"

The trees applauded.

Anika rose, stiff with cold, and thanked the Voice for its guidance and insight.

"What will you do now?" asked the Voice.

"I'm going to hire a housekeeper!" Anika laughed, "and get a massage and actually mail a letter to Corinne. But first, I'm going to relax and enjoy this mountain." Anika shook her head as she recalled all of the busy, restless days and nights and moments during the past year.

Dusk overtook the day as she walked back to the cabin with a renewed vigor. Her senses heightened by the afternoon's experience, she stopped several times to marvel at the beauty and wildlife all around her. Anika had spent so much time immersed in her letter-writing mission since she initiated her solitude all those months ago, that she'd never truly taken the time to absorb her surroundings. She was so taken with them now, that she decided she needed a vacation. Not a vacation from the mountain, but a vacation from herself, her judgments and the chatter in her mind.

There would be no more letters answered for a week, she declared, or maybe longer. Then she laughed aloud as her fingers closed on Helen's letter in her pocket once again. Well maybe just one – a really short one.

As she opened the door and stepped inside her warm, cozy cabin, her eyes fell on one of her old notebooks lying on the hearth before the dying fire. Anika was puzzled. She didn't remember placing it there. She picked it up and started flipping through the tattered pages of her old handwritten notes. As the book fell open in her hands, she gasped aloud. There, in her own handwriting, was a list of ideas for book titles that she had jotted down many years ago. One title in particular caught her eye. It read:

"If You're Going to Walk on Water, Don't Get Cold Feet!"

Anika chuckled. She had to give herself credit. Seems she really had known everything she needed to know all along – just like everyone else.

Then Anika did something she hadn't done since coming to the mountain nearly a year ago. She took off her coat, made herself a cup of peppermint tea, pulled out her laptop computer, and began to type. She didn't know what she was typing at first, but wasn't too surprised when she read:

The Frightened Messiah
A novel by:
The Writetress

"Welcome back!" said the Voice in the air around her, sounding rather pleased with itself. Anika didn't hear it. She was too busy writing.

Seeker's End

It was early on a December Saturday when Derek Shaffer pulled out of town. He was going home. He was giving up. That was it. Over. Finito. He was never going to find this woman. Once he was out of the mountains, he would call his client and apologize. He had slept in this nowhere town for nearly a month. He had walked the hills and driven the hills and talked to everyone who lived in the hills five times over. Anika Lucio simply had too much money, too much support, and was much too clever. She would be able to hide for as long as she wanted to, and Derek's deadline for completing this mission was today.

Derek was beaten and he knew it. The funny thing was, he just didn't care anymore. He hated to let his client down, but he knew he was done. He was tired of driving up and down these godforsaken mountains day after day after day. He was tired of feeling cold all the time. He was tired of the friendly mountain folk who seemed sufficiently innocent but who knew enough not to trust him with any real information. He was tired of black SUVs that seemed to disappear as if by magic whenever he got too close. Above all, he was just plain tired.

Not that he had anyplace to go really, Derek realized as he drove down the mountain on his way to . . .where? The apartment in New York was long gone. Cassandra wasn't worth chasing and Jack was off on adventures in real estate. Maybe he could start a new life somewhere too. Something fresh. Something different. He was tired of the grit of the city, tired of being a lousy, cheap P.I. who couldn't find a missing person within five miles of her own house, and tired of himself. Mostly he was tired of being Derek Shaffer, but nothing better had come to mind just yet.

Derek pulled into the only gas station he could find in some tiny dot of a town somewhere in the endless Rocky Mountains. He didn't know where he was and he didn't care. He stubbed out a cigarette in the overflowing ashtray and stepped out of the car to stretch off the hours of driving wasted. He was discouraged and depressed, but oddly numb about the whole thing. Here he had just blown the biggest case of his entire life and he couldn't even manage to care.

A late model Ford Explorer pulled up at the next pump as Derek began washing the windshield of the station wagon. It was the only other movement in the entire worthless town and it didn't matter either. He finished cleaning the front windshield and decided to skip washing the back altogether. He wasn't going to be looking behind him from now on anyway. He returned the plastic bucket of soapy water to the cement island that separated the pumps, and went back to watch the dials spin on the old, mechanical gas pump as it fed the ravenous junker he was driving. It briefly crossed his mind to wonder if the mysterious P.I. named Paul in Marina Del Rey had ever gotten what he was after.

He didn't hear her walk up behind him. Maybe because the old-fashioned gas pump whirred and clicked so loudly as it fulfilled its mission. Or maybe it was because he had started humming an odd little tune that no one had ever heard before and he was absorbed in getting it just right. Or maybe it was just plain magic. Whatever the reason, she wasn't there, until suddenly she was.

"Your name is Derek Shaffer and you've been looking for me." It was more a sympathetic statement than a question and Derek whirled around, startled from his song and yanked suddenly from his numbness.

There she was. Standing not three feet away, regarding him with a relaxed, simple smile. His heart began to pound severely. She was standing right there! He had been searching for her for months and now, when he had finally given up altogether, she had come to him. He rubbed his eyes in disbelief, his feet rooted to the ground in shock. There was nothing he could do but breathe in, breathe out, and look at her. Nothing he could do but listen to his anxious heartbeat roaring in his ears.

Aside from the fact that she appeared here out of nowhere, there was something startling about her that he had truly not experienced in any human being ever, and he didn't know quite what to do with it. Derek had seen lots of celebrities in the big city where he used to live – he couldn't quite remember its name at the moment, but there were lots of famous people living there – and what he was perceiving now was something far more than your average star-quality charisma. It was like she was sort of fuzzy around the edges somehow, but that couldn't really be. Derek rubbed his eyes again. Something about this woman was so intense and yet so gentle all at the same time, it was actually a little frightening.

She stood, in her winter coat and trademark sunglasses and waited curiously to hear what Derek had to say.

What did he have to say?

He suddenly couldn't remember why he had come. Why had he searched for this very woman all these months? He couldn't recall anything before this very moment in time and nothing else seemed to matter but right here and now.

"You've been looking for me," she repeated gently.

"Uh, yes. Yes, I have," Derek managed to stammer.

She waited. Still smiling. Still patient. Still so . . . so . . . holy in her very presence.

"I, uh, I have a message for you. It . . . it's from . . . it's from your daughter." Derek could barely form the words.

"You have a message for me from Corinne?" She was intrigued, even eager to hear what he had to say. That alone was enough encouragement to spur Derek on.

"She misses you and . . ." Derek swallowed hard, "and she wants you to come to her wedding."

"Her wedding! She and Andre are getting married?" Anika was overjoyed and her joy was more than incredible to behold. Derek began to feel as if he himself had given this perfect person, this woman who had everything money could buy and then some, the one thing she could get from no other human being on earth. The thought made him feel genuinely good inside, maybe for the first time ever. He felt positively worthy. "When is the wedding? Where?" Anika asked eagerly.

"Uh, here. I have an invitation for you." Derek's feet came unglued long enough for him to disengage the gas pump and pull open the back door of the station wagon. He rummaged impatiently through his duffel and produced the well-traveled envelope. He surfaced from inside the wagon and handed the invitation to The Writetress. In the one minute he had known her, Anika Lucio had forever become The Writetress, and he could barely remember a time when he had called her by any other name.

Derek thought she would rip open the packet from Corinne instantly, but Anika paused and held the invitation gently over her heart with both hands. She closed her eyes behind her sunglasses, and breathed very deeply. She was quiet for a long time. As he watched her curiously, Derek's own hand moved absentmindedly across his chest and he was puzzled by the hard lump in his shirt pocket. He looked down and was surprised to find a box of cigarettes in his pocket. He regarded them curiously, as though they were some strange and foreign oddity he had never seen before, then shrugged and dropped them into the trash can next to the gas pump two feet away.

"You've been looking for me for a long time," she said finally, her eyes still shut. "It has been very difficult for you."

Derek sighed deeply and looked down at the ground. He felt suddenly ashamed. There were some things he just didn't want her to know. For some strange reason, it mattered what this woman thought of him. It mattered a lot.

When he looked up, her eyes were open and she was smiling at him, her hand outstretched.

"I want to thank you. Thank you so very much," she said.

"That's o . . ." Derek reached out to take her hand and nothing was ever the same. He had a brief impression of her other arm moving up through the cold mountain air toward her face, then everything shifted into slow motion as she smiled kindly at him and removed her dark sunglasses to look deeply into his eyes. Before he knew what was happening, something unseen had sucked the breath out of his chest. The earth rushed up to meet his knees, and break his fall. Long-standing traditions of time and space were suspended as everything around him; the cars, the gas station, the pumps, leapt out at him from odd angles, in stark, jarring relief, and failed to matter all at the same time. In the space of a heartbeat, his mind was liberated from all thought and filled with all knowing. He was no longer Derek Shaffer, imperfect, jaded, rotten human being. He knew nothing but complete and perfect love and compassion for himself, for the world, and for everything and everyone in it. He was whole and he was complete, he was at peace, and he was quite happily one with the universe. All that existed was utter bliss. He never wanted anything to change, ever again. Ever.

And then his cell phone rang.

Derek snapped back to earth as The Writetress returned her sunglasses to their rightful home. The phone rang impatiently somewhere deep inside the station wagon. Derek blinked and swallowed hard. Dazed, he looked up at The Writetress. She stood, still smiling down at him with the most caring and compassionate look he had ever seen on earth. Tears of gratitude stung his eyes and he knew in that instant he would never tell another soul where she was or what had just happened to him. They could kill him if they liked, and he still wouldn't tell. He would protect her secret forever.

The phone rang again. Derek looked around in awe as if seeing the world for the first time. Everything looked different, miraculous even. The trees were sharply greener and the station sign was a bluer blue than he had ever known. Even the old station wagon looked incredible and he started to laugh out loud at the wonder of it all. He never wanted to leave this amazing gas station.

The relentless phone pierced the precious moment yet again. Derek expanded his gaze and looked around him now at the tiny town. He was still overcome by the whole experience as his eyes fell on the small diner across the street. Everything about it looked perfect and right. There was movement inside as a hand appeared for a brief moment and flipped over an OPEN sign in the door. He stared for a while before his gaze flowed to the hand-lettered sign in the window. HELP WANTED – DISH WASHER, he read, and then he smiled to himself. The phone stopped ringing. The air was still again.

"Can I help you up?" She extended her hand and Derek took it. "I've got to be going now, but I really do want to thank you again. Do you live around here?"

Derek looked slowly around at the astonishing, incredible, little mountain town again and nodded. "Yeah. Yeah. I think I do."

"Great. Maybe I'll see you around. Bye now." She climbed into her Explorer and was gone, leaving Derek standing alone, utterly and forever changed, in a small gas station, in a tiny little town, on a big green mountain in the middle of nowhere, in a very, very, very intricate, vast and perfect universe.

The End
(Or maybe, the beginning . . .)

Dear Reader,

Thank you for reading *The Writetress*. We hope you enjoyed the story. Anika Lucio herself has written an epilogue especially for this book. You may find it here: http://thewritetress.com/epilogue.

Sincerely,
The Author

Author Acknowledgements:

This project would not exist if it weren't for Drs. Ron and Mary Hulnick and the University of Santa Monica, where it was first born as part of a nine-month Self Mastery Practicum some twenty years ago. What a life-changing experience that was, and continues to be. Wow.

It wouldn't be available for you to read, if it weren't for Dr. Karen Mueller Bryson, who is an incredible writer (and podcaster!) herself, as well as being an amazing book coach and who generously advised me each step of the way; from file on my hard drive, to formatted copy with a fancy cover, to resting in your hands (or on your kindle). She also may have had a hand in helping you discover its very existence. She's that good.

And without the enthusiasm and input of readers Tamara Sumner Petersen, Candace Segar, Joel Miller, Johanna Jenkins, and Aspen Smith, I'd have almost certainly given-up on the project multiple times, which means they were instrumental in getting this book to you, too.

So, if you like the book, do thank all of the above. If not, blame me. But not too harshly, please.

The cover design is from bookcoverzone.com and they are fantastic!

Internal layout wonderfully done by adarnedgoodbook.com.

Keep track of The Writetress...

Follow the link below to sign up for occasional updates from The Writetress. Anika Lucio will let you know when she publishes something new. There is no charge or obligation and she'll never share your email address with anyone else, ever.

https://bit.ly/3vqCfFP